Ginette is a French-Canadian woman who lives in a small coastal town in Cape Breton, Nova Scotia, with her cock-a-poo, Bijou. This is Ginette's third book, in which she shares her passion for words that can easily touch your heart. She believes that words come easily from the heart when you live so close to paradise.

I dedicate this book first and foremost to God and also to all who have encouraged me, accepted me, and allowed me to walk a few steps into your lives.

Ginette Therrien

THE TRUTH IS IN THE WORDS

AUSTIN MACAULEY PUBLISHERS™
LONDON • CAMBRIDGE • NEW YORK • SHARJAH

Copyright © Ginette Therrien 2024

All rights reserved. No part of this publication may be reproduced, distributed, or transmitted in any form or by any means, including photocopying, recording, or other electronic or mechanical methods, without the prior written permission of the publisher, except in the case of brief quotations embodied in critical reviews and certain other non-commercial uses permitted by copyright law. For permission requests, write to the publisher.

Any person who commits any unauthorized act in relation to this publication may be liable to criminal prosecution and civil claims for damages.

This is a work of fiction. Names, characters, businesses, places, events, locales, and incidents are either the products of the author's imagination or used in a fictitious manner. Any resemblance to actual persons, living or dead, or actual events is purely coincidental.

Ordering Information
Quantity sales: Special discounts are available on quantity purchases by corporations, associations, and others. For details, contact the publisher at the address below.

Publisher's Cataloging-in-Publication data
Therrien, Ginette
The Truth Is in the Words

ISBN 9798889107392 (Paperback)
ISBN 9798889107408 (ePub e-book)

Library of Congress Control Number: 2023918633

www.austinmacauley.com/us

First Published 2024
Austin Macauley Publishers LLC
40 Wall Street, 33rd Floor, Suite 3302
New York, NY 10005
USA

mail-usa@austinmacauley.com
+1 (646) 5125767

Noula's Prayers

I was looking out the kitchen window when I saw her 1968 Ford T-bird turning into my driveway. She only took that car out in nice weather. It was her baby, so to speak. This was the beginning of our special weekend. It could turn out to be a blessing or a disaster. My head was swimming with the surge of adrenaline coursing through my body. As soon as her foot hit the pavement, I opened the door and waited for her.

"Jacks, you look great! You seem different. What has happened to you that the stress has left your face? What has changed? You even look years younger. You met someone! It's so nice to see you. I've missed you so much!"

Those were the first words flying out of Fran's mouth as she kept me at arm's length, looking at me straight in the eyes, before we sat down after a long hug. I had not seen Fran in seven years. Our lives were busy, and we lived miles apart, and not only physically speaking. Fran ran her own consulting business and traveled all over Canada and the United States. She was even hired by some European firms who wanted to learn how to better utilize what they had as stock and staff with more efficiency. She was a self-made efficiency expert. She was gifted in her field. Francine Ester

Poulin, aka Fran, was respected in the corporate world and considered a genius at her job.

Her personal life was not as successful. She was married to her business with little time to give to anything or anyone else. She didn't stay in relationships for very long. Her heart had been broken a long time ago, which never mended, and that's what caused her to submerge herself in her work. She kept herself too busy for feelings or regrets. It took her many years to come to terms with the loss of her heart, but when she got her footing back, nothing could stop her. She was in control of her business and of her life.

Me? I am Jacqueline Anne Nenacks. Jackie to most and Jacks to Fran. Fran and I have been friends since I was six, and she was five. We were neighbors in rural Grand River, in Cape Breton. We laughed together and cried together, we got in and out of trouble together, and we fought like siblings. Our parents had their own lives, which didn't include us much. Between work, booze, and their social lives, they barely had time to sleep. It didn't matter to us at the time. We were free to do whatever we wanted. We only found out later in life the price that our childhood cost us.

Fran and I drifted apart and came back together throughout the years, but we were always just a call away. We could read each other's minds; that's how close we've always been. That's the reason I invited her here for the weekend to share with her something which changed my life and, if I tell it right, will change Fran's life as well. One of the reasons is that I needed her to hear what I had to say, and she really needed to hear it.

"NO! I have not met someone. Not really, not in the way you think. What kind of 'HELLO' is that anyway? What makes you think that I have changed? I see you're still the same, direct, no-nonsense let's get down to it!

I can't believe you're really here and that we have an entire weekend to catch up on seven-plus years. I have missed you so much! When did you get back from London? I think it's been over a year since we even spoke on the phone for more than a few minutes."

"I got back six weeks ago, but I have been behind in my local contracts and busy hiring a new assistant who will travel with or for me. I can't do it all by myself anymore, especially when I'm traveling. Julie runs the office when I'm away and does a bang-up job, and the others respect her, but I know she's overworked as well, and I've been negligent in getting her some proper help. I gave Julie the go-ahead to hire herself an assistant.

So, what has been happening with you, and who has put that spark in your eyes?"

"As you know, I accepted a position closer to home and for a lot more money last February. I don't have to travel two hours to get to work. I am now Head of Nursing at Sunset Haven Nursing Home, a seniors' residence here in the village of Arichat. I love everything about the changes in my life. I have so much to tell you and doubt that the weekend will give us enough time to take it all in.

How's Ben these days?"

"Ben left me four weeks ago. Packed his stuff and moved out while I was in London. I know I should have told you sooner, but time got away, like I said, and I put it on the back burner until I had time to process it myself. I wish that I could say I was surprised, but that would not be accurate. I'm not even that upset about it. He said that he was tired of being alone in my house, waiting to be a part of my life all in my time and on my terms. He left me this letter along with my key."

I had only heard a little about Ben. He was the latest failed convenience, so to speak. Fran met him at the airport in New Orleans while traveling for work. They had shared a cab ride to the same hotel, as it turned out. She was a guest speaker at a conference hosted by Briggs Inc., and Ben was attending it. When they returned to New Brunswick, they kept seeing each other whenever they could. According to my calculations, it lasted eight months.

"I'm sorry Fran; I know that you loved him as best you could, that is, and from his words, he knew it too. Sounds like you still have a good friend in Ben, though. I'm sure he meant every word."

"Enough about me; what is going on with you? You look so content."

I must admit that I was nervous about the outcome of this weekend. Fran has always been hard to pin down when it comes to sharing emotions and feelings. She avoided those conversations at all costs. She walked out on me while on vacation 30 years ago because I dared ask her a too-close-to-the-heart question. When she came back to the hotel room, I made sure to keep it light.

"Like I mentioned to you, I love my new job. I started in my new position on Valentine's Day. The staff is very easy to work with, and I have no complaints so far. It's still the honeymoon period, so to speak. Basically, it's just a normal everyday routine with no surprises so far. I do, however, have something interesting and important as well, to share with you, but you can't get spooked and leave. Just hear me out."

"I want to hear it all, of course. We have a lot to catch up on, for sure!

Did you know that Aunt Frieda passed away? I would have liked to attend her funeral, but I couldn't make it work. I called Melissa and talked to her for over an hour on the phone from St Andrews, Scotland, and I sent flowers."

"Yes, I even went to your aunt Frieda's funeral. It was last June, right? Melissa was happy to see me. She was glad I went. There weren't many people there. I stayed after the luncheon and visited with your cousin for a while. She seemed so alone. Didn't we end up talking about the time Melissa had asked me to go check on her mom? Remember, there was a blizzard, and Melissa was stuck in Sydney. Seeing as I was only a few blocks away, I agreed to drive over to check on her. Melissa was worried about her mother because her dementia was getting worrisome. She had been diagnosed with late-stage Alzheimer's. She hated to leave her alone on a good day, let alone during a storm."

"I don't think you told me about that. What happened, and where was I?"

"It was around two years ago. I was working at the General in Sydney, and I believe you were in Madrid at the time. It was your first contract in Madrid if I remember correctly. I thought for sure I had shared that with you?"

"Share it with me now. I love hearing stories about Aunt Frieda."

"Like I said, it was during a blizzard. I barely made it to her house. I got stuck in the driveway as soon as I drove in and had to walk to the door from near the road. The snow was almost to my knees. It had been snowing since early morning, and it wasn't slowing down by evening. When I knocked at the front door, all I heard was loud music, so I banged harder on the door until Freida finally opened it. She was all out of breath, and when she saw it was me, she called me by name and gave me a big hug as though I was a long-lost loved one. I thought she would not have recognized me because Melissa had told me how affected Frieda was by her dementia, but she knew exactly who I was and ushered me out of the storm. She offered me a cup of tea, which I gladly accepted, and hung my coat on the hall tree behind the door while I put my boots near the heat register to keep them warm. She then went to the closet and came back with a pair of pliers. I was seated at the kitchen table watching her when I noticed that the knobs were missing on the stove. I said, "Frieda, what happened to your burner knobs?" She looked at me with a smile and said that Melissa had forbidden her to use the stove when she was not home and hid the knobs. She then turned the burner on under the kettle.

After a short exchange of pleasantries, she motioned for me to follow her to the back sun porch. She said that she wanted to show me something interesting. She opened the outside door, leaned out, and pointed at something in the distance, so I leaned forward to see what it was she wanted me to see. As I was halfway out, looking at where she had pointed, she pushed me out into the storm and closed and locked the door. There I was, outside in a blizzard, in my stocking feet with no coat and with my keys in the house and my car over twenty feet away stuck in the snow. I fought my way back to the front porch, hoping she would let me in long enough to at least get my stuff. I knocked on the door a couple of times when Frieda opened it with a surprised look on her face and said, "Jackie, how very nice to see you. It's been forever. Come in, come in. I just put the kettle on for tea. Would you like a cup?"

When I told Melissa what had happened, that's when she decided that Frieda couldn't stay alone anymore."

"I can't…I can't believe she threw you out the back door in the storm. Hahahahah, that's hysterical. Hahahah. What did you do when she let you back in?"

"I stayed until the roads were open and Melissa made it home. We sat at the kitchen table and had tea then I took the liberty of making us something to eat. Then when it got late, she just got up and went to bed. I left after Melissa made it home around midnight."

"Melissa was horrified when I told her what had happened, but she didn't have any difficulty laughing her face off when we were reminiscing about it the day of the funeral. It felt good to remember Frieda. I used to check up on her as much as I could until there was a place for her in a nursing home. Her dementia progressed so fast. I'm surprised, though, at how long she lasted in the nursing home."

"Aunt Frieda was a character. She loved life and shared every moment of it with Bernie, her husband. They were spontaneous and playful. They got arrested on their honeymoon for streaking up and down the stairs of St Joseph Oratory in Montreal. I'm sure the people who were there on a pilgrimage praying for a miracle got a big surprise. I could write a book on their antics and adventures. They were so well suited to each other.

Frieda was my favorite out of all of them. Her brother, Uncle Wilfred, was always protective of her, but Uncle Larry was mean. When Wilfred wasn't around, Larry picked on her until she would cry. Grandma was a single mom at a young age, and Wilfred tried to help as much as he could. Larry resented not having a father. He was the youngest. My dad was the oldest. Dad left the house at a young age to work and sent money to Grandma to help her. He was only home on holidays. He also protected Frieda from Larry when he was around. Dad gave Larry a beating one time, which scared Larry, and he left Frieda alone then. Larry died in a car accident when he was twenty-five. He was drunk and lost control of his truck and hit a tree."

"I truly liked Frieda. She was a gentle soul. Too bad you couldn't make it to her funeral. Melissa would have loved to see you. Are you in touch with anyone in your family?"

"I saw them all at the Poulin family reunion over two years ago. Frieda wasn't her playful self. She was different after Uncle Bernie passed away. I believe her heart died with him.

I haven't seen or talked to anyone on my mother's side in forever. We were never close. All I have left are cousins, which I never really knew. After Mom died, none of them made any effort to stay in touch.

I've known you long enough, Jacks, to know that you have a reason for insisting I come here this weekend. What's going on? Must be very important that I could not say no."

"I do have a lot to share, and it is very important that you listen to every story and not get impatient. When all is said, you'll understand why I took that route. To make sure you don't get bored, I got us a few bottles of your favorite Australian cab-sauv and a bottle of cognac if you get restless.

It all started at the regional hospital before I got this job. I thought nothing of it at the time, not until I met and spent a lot of time with Noula-May Fortier. Noula.

On my last week at the Regional, one quiet Sunday morning in the wee hours, the ambulance brought this elderly man to emergency with a code blue. He was in rough shape, to say the least. They revived him, and he then went into a coma shortly after. He was dying of liver failure. To me, it was another ordinary shift, and my day went on. The man was put on a liver transplant list but with very poor odds of getting a liver seeing as he was nameless homeless drunk. He slipped out of the coma the last day I was there. No one came to visit him or inquire about him. There was something about him that nagged at me, but I dismissed it and moved on to my new job where I am now. I had not thought about the homeless man until shortly before Noula passed away.

Noula was a few years older than we are. She was a resident at the seniors' home where I now work. She had been brought in for a month of respite care and ended up becoming a permanent resident due to the fact that she was totally blind and in poor health.

Noula loved to tell stories. She would blurt out a story out of nowhere. I would sit with her even after my shifts. I saw myself going in on my days off just to listen to her. I absolutely loved her. Because of her and her stories, I have changed, like you said, and I am at peace like never before. By the time I get to the final story, you will be as well. This is life-changing, Fran. So, before I get into it, let's get a bite to eat at The Charter restaurant, then get comfy with a glass of wine. It's a lot to take in."

"I was getting used to my new duties and getting to know my staff and the residents. I have a good crew working for me, and the residents love them. Everyone gets along really well. Tuesday, after the Easter long weekend, we had a woman come to us for respite care. That's when I met Noula-May Fortier, like I said, Noula. She was only supposed to stay at the home for a month while her assisted living apartment was ready for her. You see, Noula was completely blind, but in reasonably good health, so it seemed. The first week she was with us, I noticed that her breathing became labored with the slightest effort. I told the resident doctor what I had observed, and he then ordered a battery of tests. While waiting for the results of those tests to come in, life went on as normal, and I got to know her a little better. She didn't speak about herself, but she loved sharing short stories she had experienced. It was a roundabout way of getting to know her. She said that the only things in life which were truly important are the stories that have touched us or taught us something that we must share. The rest is boring filler. I was really drawn to her.

Noula would spend her alone time in prayer. When I came into her room, she would engage in conversation, but if I stuck around a bit longer, she would tell me a story. My first experience with Noula's storytelling touched me, and I wanted to hear more. She spoke of a little girl's tears which still made her cry even after over 45 plus years. The little girl, Sally, had wanted a kitten for a very long time. She was an only child and always alone. Her mother would always say no to Sally. She kept asking her mother with pleading tears for a kitten, but the answer was always a stern no. Noula, who lived next door and befriended Sally, went over one day and talked to Sally's mother in the hope of convincing her to allow Sally to have a kitten and that she would even buy her one herself. Finally, her mother gave in and allowed Noula to get her a kitten. The day after that, Sally's mother said yes. Noula showed up at her house with a tiny kitten. Sally cried tears of joy that day. She had been a lonely little girl, but the kitten filled her loneliness by giving her love a place to go. She called the little grey and white kitten Kitty.

Kitty was the first thing on Sally's mind when she awoke and the last thing before falling asleep. Noula could hear Sally talking to Kitty in the backyard, and she would watch her from her kitchen window. Sally would hug and kiss Kitty and keep her in her arms, rocking Kitty like a mother rocking her baby.

One day Sally was calling for Kitty to come inside. As she was calling Kitty's name and watching for her, Kitty darted in front of a car, and Sally ran screaming towards the car just as the car ran over Kitty. Kitty died right away. Noula still heard Sally's screams from deep inside her, and the tears instantly flowed after all those years. Noula said that she had never heard such anguish. Sally didn't speak for weeks. Not a word! It was the saddest thing to watch. Noula felt so guilty, because if it were not for her involvement, Sally would never have gone through such pain.

Noula then closed her eyes and started praying again. I quietly left her room with tears running down my face. It marked me, Fran. The way she told it. The story itself. The look on her face. It was as though she was there again and took me with her. She went into such detail and such depth.

I went into Noula's room after my shift at 7 pm to check on her and to find out what happened to Sally. Noula had a distant smile on her face and said that Sally went on being lonely and never asked for another kitten. Her mother was not the warmest person, which didn't help. She didn't even console Sally the day she lost Kitty. Sally grew up to be a very depressed woman. Her mother was an alcoholic as well, which didn't help Sally in her life. The last I heard; Sally had moved in with this bully of a man who didn't treat her right either. She died at the young age of 24 by suicide. Her mother drank herself to death shortly after.

I was numb. I said my goodbyes and went home. Noula still carried Sally's pain with her, and now, so do I. It's the strangest thing, Fran. It's now a story that I own, just as though I was there. I can't explain the effect that Noula had on me. It's never happened to me before."

"What did Noula do in life?"

"Please don't ask questions. I can't stray from the way I'm telling you all of this. You'll know all about her, I promise. Please don't ask any more questions, and keep an open mind. Sit back and enjoy your wine. It's really important, Fran, that I don't deviate from my plan in sharing all this. I have given this hour, mulling this over in my head until I was ready to say what I have to say. You have to trust me."

I saw the look on Fran's face. A look of fight or flight. I had to tread carefully. Fran was suspicious of everyone and everything. She was the most difficult person to pin down, especially when it got too serious. And this was going to get very serious!

"In my line of work, you hear a lot of stories and see things unique to my position. When people move into these homes, all they have left are stories of the lives they have lived. They know that this is their last home and the only way out is death. You get used to the stories and the loneliness. Most residents are abandoned by their families, or they have outlived them all and are the only ones left with stories they want to leave behind so they will be remembered by someone. All they have are memories if they're fortunate enough to remember them. The minutes tick away in their heads like resounding gongs. It's difficult to watch at times. That's why it's so important to take time and listen to them even when it makes no sense sometimes. I must admit, though, that Noula has brought that to my heart more than anyone I have ever known. I wish that I could explain it better.

As I said before, the people that I work with are great. They treat the residents with respect and humor. They go out of their way to put a smile on their face and make them feel important. They make sure that the residents feel at home and comfortable. One of the RPNs, Jen, makes them special desserts on their birthdays and brings that special treat, which she makes at home on her own time and dime, to work. Another staff member, Kirk, will bring his guitar to work every now and then, and give them a little concert and sing-along. The residents tap into the music, and some even get up and dance a few steps. It doesn't take much to make them happy for a while. Just like it doesn't take long to see the loneliness come back and their eyes go blank."

Noula liked to stay in her room. She always had the music playing low and sat in her rocking chair with the window open on nice days to hear the waves. Her light was always left on for us, but she was not aware of it because of her blindness. It was for us, not her. Noula lost her sight all at once about two years ago, I believe. It had been failing for a while, but then with no warning, the light was gone just like that. Though she knew it was going to happen that way, it was still hard to adjust to when it finally happened. I'll touch on that later. I really don't want to get ahead of myself.

The results from all the tests that the doctor had ordered were in. Noula was dying of a progressive heart deterioration. She had a couple of months at best. This particular heart disease is quick, and most patients pass away peacefully in their sleep. It's the only good thing about it.

I was the one who was with the doctor when he broke the news to her. I think we felt worse for her than she did. She thanked us for the information and assured us that this was not bad news. She was, after all, a woman with a strong faith. As we exited her room, I heard her starting to pray. No. Not praying. It was praise. Somehow, she knew that I was still standing near her door inside her room. All she said was, "I'm fine, Nurse Nenacks. Really, I am. God is always with me. I'm looking forward to seeing Him again." I was floored!"

"Wait a minute, Jacks. Are you one of those "born-again people now?" Is that why I'm here? What is this? I'm not feeling too comfortable with all this. You know me and the "God thing." I'm not going to be swayed. Not even by you!"

"I'm not trying to convert you. Hear me out, please! I'm asking you again to be patient and listen with an open mind. You have no idea where this is all going. You know me enough to trust me. Please, Fran. You have no idea how important this is."

"Ok, but I'll need another glass of wine. I do trust you, Jacks, and I will listen. I just felt uncomfortable with what was being said. It's been a long time and a rough road for me. Now that I have my wine, please continue."

Fran had been hurt a lot at a young age. We both had it hard. Fran had the worst of it. I could cope better with all that was happening, but Fran went inside herself and still to this day. The last push that pushed her farther inside was done by a priest at our church when she was seventeen. She was in trouble. That's what they called it back then. She went to him to ask for guidance and his help. She had not trusted anyone but me in a long while. After she had told him what was wrong, he drove her home and told her parents that she was pregnant. He betrayed her in her most vulnerable time.

Her parents were both drunk, as always, and her father laid a beating on her when he heard, while her mother called her names at the top of her lungs and all in front of this priest. Fran never went back to church and, to this day, still blames God for not helping her. She never forgave her parents for their reaction. Her mother died about a year later, and her father quit drinking and became one of those "born-again" people. That pushed Fran even further away.

"I was off the next day, but I had to go see Noula. It was after lunch when I arrived. Noula was sitting in her rocker, listening to her music. She had a look of peace about her.

She almost beamed. I bought each of us a blueberry muffin and a coffee from Robin's. She was happy for the treat and the company. We barely said a word while we had our collation. I felt as comfortable as I do with you. Noula was the one to break the silence with this story."

"You know, I used to love going to Point Michaud beach. Especially when the weather kept other people away, this one day, in mid-September, during a light rain, I went for a walk along the beach. I was alone and loving it. I did my best thinking there. Not long into my walk, I saw a gannet, a beautiful gull-like bird, who was trying to fly but looked too weak to get off the ground. I watched him for a while to see what was going on with this poor bird. The longer I stood there watching, the more evident it was that the bird was struggling and was in serious trouble. I was horrified. I took my wind-breaker off and walked slowly toward the frightened, failing bird. He tried to fly and run from me, but he was too weak. I finally caught him and wrapped him gently in my jacket. I then quickly walked to my car with tears blinding my every step. My heart was heavy with pain for this poor beast. It had a fishing line hanging from its mouth, and I could see a hook inside. My anger and hatred surfaced violently. This poor creature was suffering because of a careless human being.

I had no cell service where I was, so I drove like a bat out of hell to get help. When my cell phone finally had coverage, I called my mechanic, Bob. His neighbor was a vet. I asked him to call the vet at his house and that I was on my way with a bird who needed attention, and that I would be there in twenty minutes. He could tell I was upset. Bob agreed to call Dr. Howe and ask him for his help.

I looked at the bird often while driving to see how it was doing. Poor thing had sand lice running all over its head and back. I cursed those bugs. When I arrived at Bob's, Dr. Howe was waiting for us with his little black bag on the tailgate of his truck. Bob came quickly to get the bird from the car. Dr. Howe opened its mouth and gently tugged on the fishing line. He then turned to me and said that the line had multiple hooks and that the bird had swallowed them. There was nothing he could do to save it. He then opened his bag and took out a needle to euthanize the suffering bird. I couldn't stay to watch. I didn't even say goodbye or thank you. I could barely breathe. I sobbed all the way home. I cried for days every time I would see the gannet in my mind. It took me a few weeks before I could go back to Bob's and thank him and his wife for their help. I knew that Dr. Howe lived next door, so I brought him a nice potted aster I had purchased at the nearby nursery to show my appreciation, and I also wanted to pay him for his work. He said that the aster was more than enough and that he was glad he could help.

So, you see, Nurse Nenacks, that people can be both good, thoughtful, and helpful, but they are also selfish, destructive, and harmful."

"I reached out my hand and touched hers. I said how sorry I was that she had to see that poor bird suffer but how lucky it was that because of her, its suffering was not for long. I also told her to call me Jackie. She smiled then she looked at me as though she could see inside my head. I was sitting there across from her with tears streaming down my face again. Her stories were both heart-wrenching and heart-healing. Both are emotional. Just as I was going to say something, Noula started praying as though I had left. I quietly got up and took my leave.

I went home and made myself a cup of coffee, and sat in front of my window overlooking the ocean. Why would Noula share such random stories, and why did they affect me so deeply? There was no reasonable explanation. I decided to let it go, and I turned the stereo on and did housework. I was okay. So, I thought.

It got weird again later on. My mind would not let go of Noula and her stories. I found myself crying over Sally's dead kitten, and my heart was hurting for the dying gannet. Why was I being so sensitive all of a sudden? I allowed myself a good cry and let it go. I must have needed a release, and Noula's stories gave it to me."

"Monday morning, after our staff meeting, I went to see Noula. She seemed happy I was there. She asked me to come back after my shift if I wasn't too tired. I told her that I would be there around 7 pm.

That same day we lost a resident, Mr. Linden. When I went to his room to make sure his body was ready for transport, I found Noula in there sitting on the side of his bed, and she was holding his hand and talking to him. I heard her say to Mr. Linden, "I'm so happy for you, Simon. You're going to be so happy there. No one will ever take the love away ever again." She then said to me, "he's gone home and left this behind." She was referring to his body. I didn't even know that she knew I was there. Then she got up from his bed and felt her way out of his room, and went on to hers.

I had questions. Many questions. I went to Noula's room after work and sat next to her. She asked me why I was so perplexed. The question stunned me. How could she know how I looked or felt? She didn't even wait for an answer. She instead told me another story. Now I knew that she was "all there," so to speak. I never questioned her mental capacities and abilities. I just didn't understand the woman at all. Yet I was drawn to her. This is the story she shared with me that day. ``

"There was this magnificent storm cloud covering the entire sky to the east, and it looked like it was barely touching the ocean. It was a warm November day with no wind, but the waves were still angry. They sounded like thunder when they fought each other to shore and retreated back to their vastness with a whisper. I was alone, enjoying everything which touched my senses. I felt God's presence that day. I often felt Him when the majesty of His creations touched me.

As I walked along the shore, I found a few sand dollars pushed by the waves onto the beach and shells of all different sizes. Like I said, I was totally enjoying myself until I came upon a dying seal. At first, I thought that he was already dead, but then he moved ever so slightly. My breath caught in my throat, and my heart broke for him. Then I saw the beauty of it. There he was, lying in the sand away from the shore. All was peaceful, and he was so very calm. He made dying look poetic and peaceful. I felt like I was intruding on something so precious and personal. I felt God's presence ever stronger. All of a sudden, my heart was filled with rage. I saw the bullet hole in his neck on the right side. He had been shot and had come to shore to die. Some fisherman had shot him. It was common practice for them to shoot seals when they were lobster fishing. It was so very wrong! The hatred and anger took over my senses for a fleeting moment. I did not allow the ugliness of my thoughts and feelings to take away from this special experience for long. So, I praised God and said a prayer for this gift which he was sharing with me, and I turned and walked away, giving the seal the privacy and the dignity he deserved. It felt as though nature was comforting him. The waves were sharing their song, the clouded sky was covering him, and a gentle breeze was showing him the way home. It was a magical moment.

As I was walking back to the car, I needed to sit. I was a little shaken. There was a bench in the tall grass halfway to the car. I was sitting in nature's beauty when I saw three people walking toward where I was. We greeted each other briefly, and they continued on. I watched them as they spotted the dying seal. They stopped near it and stared for a few moments. I was too far away to hear what they were saying. Then the man in the group walked over to the seal and kicked it. I had never felt more disgust for another human being in all my life. I just let out a primal scream, got up, and left. I was never a fan of humans to start off with, and seeing this shameless person take away the dignity of the seal's final moments was more than my heart could take. I had to leave. I could not trust myself not to do something I would regret later. I wanted to hurt this man with all my physical power. My hatred ran deep.

When I got to my car, I lost my rage, and my heart felt at peace. I then realized that God was helping me cope with what I had just seen. He then showed me that the seal was with Him. All I could do was praise God.

Then it was as though I wasn't there anymore, and she started praying. So, I quietly got up, ready to leave, when she asked me to come again tomorrow. I agreed, said good night, and left.

I couldn't figure out why Noula was telling me these stories and then afterward retreating inside her prayers. I wanted to know why! Next day at work, I asked some of the other staff if Noula shared stories with any of them. They all said no. I asked them if she shared stories or visited anyone else that they were aware of. Not that they had seen was their reply. Susan, the occupational therapist, came to me a few minutes later and told me that Noula had told her that she was praying for her situation at home and that all would work out for the best. She said that Noula told her that out of the blue. I asked Susan if Noula knew her and if she was right. Susan assured me that there was no way that she could know anything about her and her private life. Then Susan told me that her husband had been fired from his position at the fish plant, but out of nowhere, he had received a call from Brass Industries and was given a job, and for better pay. How did Noula know that?

I avoided Noula's room the rest of the morning. I had meetings away from Sunset Haven in the afternoon, so even if I wanted to visit with her, my schedule would not allow it. When I got home from my meetings, it was past 8 pm. It was a long day, and I was tired and cranky from dealing with closed-minded people all afternoon. I poured myself a glass of wine and made myself a sandwich. I had just sat down when the phone rang. It was the home. Noula was asking for me. I told Robin, the night shift nurse, that I would see her in the morning. Robin then informed me that

Noula didn't look well, and she was concerned about her. I told her that I would be right there.

I arrived at the home within minutes and found Noula propped up in bed. She looked tired and pale. I announced that I was there and asked her why she wanted to see me. Robin came in shortly after I arrived with Noula's chart to show me her vitals. After looking at the chart, I told Robin to call the doctor. Noula flatly refused. She said that it could wait until proper working hours and that the doctor needed his rest. That tied my hands. I could not convince her to change her mind.

I sat in Noula's rocking chair and waited for her to speak. I was surprised at what happened next. I didn't expect the comment that came from her. She said, "Jackie, I want you to know that I understand why people are such a disappointment to you and the pain which created such feelings." I was speechless. She then said, "I recognize the anger."

I had not shown anger or resentment, or any negative emotion around any residents or staff, or Noula. You know me, Fran, I'm pretty even keel. So, I asked her what she meant by that. Then she opened up in a very unexpected and personal way."

"Jackie, you and I are very much alike. I have carried anger and hatred with me all of my life, and like you, I have never used it to hurt anyone. With age and strength, we learned to live with what was imposed on us, even when it went against our very own gentle nature. Life has humbled us, and we were wise enough to see this as a gift. We have learned to turn this cancerous hatred and use it to safely walk through life the best we could. I feel the gentleness in you. When those hard emotions go against our God-given nature, and we still have the capacity to love, it makes us conquerors.

It was hard losing our mother at a young age. It left my brother, Paul, and I with just our father to care for us. Dad never recovered from losing his wife to heart failure at the age of 37. It seems like I have inherited her heart condition.

Dad was a good man, but what did he know about raising two kids on his own? He worked 40 hours a week at the mill, and my mother did everything else. When she died, he didn't know how to cook or what to cook. Mother had done it all. The shopping, cooking, cleaning, banking, and raising us. He was a lost soul.

I was seven, and Paul was five when we lost her. Needless to say, that I grew up quickly. I knew more about what to do than Dad did, but I was too young to take charge. Dad hired Mrs. Belanger to care for us and him as well. She was our neighbor. She had lost her husband before we had moved there five years prior. She was a single mom to Jerry, her useless son. He was a mean and devious teenager. But in her eyes, he could do no wrong.

Paul and I would go to Mrs. Belanger's house after school until our dad came to collect us. I would make breakfast for us and get us ready for school, then Dad would take us next door, and he would leave for work. We had an hour of wait until the bus would arrive to take us to school and another hour with Mrs. Belanger after the bus dropped us off after school. She would have dinner ready for us to take home when Dad arrived. It wasn't long before we fell into a robotic routine. Our lives felt lifeless, with no show of emotions of joy or visible sadness. Routine, robotic routine.

Jerry started molesting me soon after we were being cared for by Mrs. Belanger. She didn't notice anything. Her afternoons were spent in front of the TV watching soap operas. Jerry would take me to his room and force me to perform things on him, and he would also hurt me. I couldn't tell anyone because he promised to hurt Paul if I said a word. To prove that he meant his threat, he punched Paul in the face and lied about it convincingly to his mother and our father. Like I said, in his mother's eyes, he could do no wrong. He bullied Paul every chance he had. More than once, Paul would carry bruises, mostly hidden ones. Jerry was a monster.

Nobody noticed that we were being abused. People just thought that we were sad due to the tragic loss of our mother. Thank God that we didn't stay long under Mrs. Belanger's care. Dad met Sarah, and they got married nine months after our mother died. Sarah loved Dad. She loved him all right but resented us. She wanted him for herself. Though she wasn't abusive towards us, she made it clear that she wanted us to be invisible and quiet. She pretended to like us when Dad was within earshot, but the minute she had her chance, she would send us away."

"I then interrupted her. I said, with a shakiness in my voice, "Noula, you must be exhausted. Do you want to stop for now, and we can get together tomorrow if you like?" She gave a slight nod and started praying as I got up to leave."

"I don't get it, Jacks. What is this woman doing? Out of nowhere, she tells you stories and now talks about her life and says that you and her are alike in some way. What made her think that you had a commonality with her?"

"It's not hard to understand Fran. She's all alone and without sight. Plus, she's living in a nursing home with a death sentence looming. It makes perfect sense that she would be sensitive to her surroundings. What I don't understand is why she seems to know things about me, and she's been accurate in her assumptions. Maybe she has a sixth sense. I just have not figured out why she has chosen me. When people are dying, they choose someone to share their thoughts and feelings. A lot of the time, they choose strangers. Noula made it clear that she wanted to be remembered and mourned by me. It's an honor, really, when you think about it.

I went in an hour earlier to work the next day to clear time in my calendar for a few days. I wanted to be available for Noula whenever she wanted to share. At around ten, after rounds, meds. and morning routine was over, and I popped in to say good morning to her. She looked rested and pleased to see me. She asked if I could sit with her while she had her breakfast. She had requested a late one, and it had just arrived. I pulled up the chair from the corner and sat, ready for a trip through Noula's life.

We started out with small talk. The usual. Weather, what I did last evening when I returned home, and then she started again."

"Life went on, and we grew up carrying our memories and scars. At a young age, we don't feel the weight of the baggage that we are accumulating. We think that everything is as it's supposed to be. We don't know how to look outside ourselves and see how others are living. One day though, it hits you that maybe it was harder than it should have been, which lets the anger and the hatred take root.

Nonetheless, we grew up, and we fell in and out of love. We learned about things and moved forward. Paul fell in love with Eve, and they got married and settled down in the next village from where we grew up in Cape Breton, Nova Scotia. As for me, I never married; I went to school and became a legal secretary, got a job at Tate & Beaton law firm in Sydney, and moved to Mira. Three years ago, I started working closer to my roots at a law office in Port Hawkesbury and took an apartment here in Arichat.

Dad and Sarah moved to Niagara Falls, where Sarah had come from. Dad died four years later of cancer at the age of 76. We never heard from our stepmom after the funeral. She didn't bother with us, nor did we bother with her. We had never been close. I respected her as my father's wife, and that was enough.

My first month at the law firm of Tate & Beaton, I did meet someone I believed I could love. His name was William. He was a law student in the office, and I was to be his secretary as well. We would have lunch in the lunchroom almost every day. We even started seeing each other outside of work. Nothing serious at first; we were just friends. Our relationship started to progress slowly. We held hands and kissed goodnight at my door. We went for long rides and picnics. We were comfortable companions. He was kind and patient. One evening while we were sitting waiting for the movie to start at the drive-in theatre, William tearfully admitted that he was gay and apologized to me for using me as his front; his beard is what he called it. It eased his mind a great deal when I said that I truly enjoyed his friendship and company and that I was quite happy with the arrangement as it stood. We stayed friends until he passed away in 2007. He had been married for twelve years to Johnathan Taylor when he died. Johnathan passed away last year. He was a good friend as well to the end.

"Can I ask you a personal question, Jackie?"

"Yes, of course, you can. Go ahead, ask away."

"How did you feel after the three stories I shared with you? Am I right to assume that you felt them deeply, and now you feel like you own them?"

"First of all, they showed me a part of you that was intriguing to me, and yes, I feel like I do own them now. I want to know more about you because of them, and now you've opened your life to me, which tells me I was right. As for the three stories themselves? Well, the story about Sally and her kitten made me cry and hurt for the little girl. You brought me straight to her pain. It brought back memories of my life in Grand River. I had found a kitten dead behind the shed when I was ten. It had been poisoned by the neighbor. I cried as I buried it in the field next to the oak tree.

The story about the gannet showed me a side of you which brought me to your pain, and the seal showed me your contempt for humans and your love of animals. I have to admit that I felt instant hatred for the man who kicked at the seal as well. I might not have had your control, though. All three stories touched me deeply and made me cry. Is that why you told me about them? To see my reactions?"

"Let me explain to you what they mean to me. I was a hateful, angry person who had lost faith in mankind. I couldn't understand the selfishness and its cost to others and the violence and the abuse imposed on the innocent and the defenseless. I stayed away from people, which also meant that I didn't have many friends. The friends I have made in life were merely acquaintances and neighbors. I was disillusioned with humans, but I always felt close to God. God says that if we can't love humans, then how could we love him whom we cannot see? My argument was that it is because we can see what human beings are capable of, which makes it difficult to love them.

Sally and the kitten was a difficult one to understand. The odds were against this child, given the mother she had and the loneliness which consumed her. The only beauty in Sally's life was the kitten and what it brought to the child. I was crushed when her little heart was broken with the loss of Kitty. I felt so responsible. I saw no good at all in that experience. God showed me that for a fleeting moment in Sally's life, she knew pure love and happiness and that if it were not for me, she would have missed that. He also showed me that Sally's mother was so broken by the loss of the child she ignored because, in her own way, she loved her and drank herself to death. The woman could not cope with life.

The gannet. To see that beautiful bird grounded by pain, too weak to run or fly because of man's negligence. I questioned God that day. Why do we destroy all the beauty that you have given us with little to no regard for life? Though it wasn't a malicious attempt at harming the bird, it was still due to some careless human actions. Then in my rage, I called for help from another person. I saw my anger. I saw the bird's pain and fear. I also saw human compassion. That's what I needed to see. God reaches us so individually.

He used anger and pain to show me love. I wasn't the only one with a broken heart for the bird. My eyes were not the only ones with tears streaming from them.

The most difficult one for me was the seal. It brought out every emotion in me. I saw the ugliness in my own rage and hatred when I realized the gift of the moment. It was poetic. I could almost hear a choir of angels soothing the seal with song and the waves a symphony in the background as though to free it of any fear and pain in his last moments. I actually saw the hatred I carry with me daily. So, I thanked God for showing me that I, the human, was the ugliness in the moment of beauty. But then the rage came back, and this time God showed me that my anger was righteous anger. It was justified. It was heartless of the man to kick at the poor beast. He showed me my anger with no sin.

All three experiences have been a reminder to me that I am a flawed human being with a passion to love and hate but not harm. They may not mean much to anyone else, but to you and me, I know they touch and teach the heart. Am I right, Jackie?"

I also wanted to know you better as well and see if I could trust you with much more. Seeing as time is not on my side, and I went for your heart. I have things to say before God takes me home. Things that He wants me to say, and I think he wants me to say them to you. All I ask is that you listen. These words, like all words, are important. Words are powerful weapons to hurt, help, and heal. I don't believe in wasting them. They're far too precious, especially when they are laid on your heart to share.

I have given you something to think about. Come by when you have had time to mull over what has been said and when you have time to sit with me for a while. You'll understand everything when I'm done, and even why those words were shared. Please trust me."

"Then, like she always did, Noula started to pray, and I was dismissed. I was hooked. I needed to find out more. My curiosity was peaked. I went and looked at Noula's file again to see if there was anyone or any information which could enlighten me. The only other name in her file was Angel Tanguay, an address in Petit de Grat with no phone number. Relationship "granddaughter." She must have had a child out of wedlock. She had just told me that she never married. I was so consumed with all she had shared, along with her demeanor, her stories, and her peace. I wish you could have met her, Fran.

Well, I need a break. Let's go for a walk and an Ice cream. It's too nice an evening to spend it all cooped up inside."

"I can see that this woman really got to you, Jacks. You got me intrigued as well. When did she die?"

"She passed away a week ago yesterday. I was with her when she passed. It was one of the most peaceful deaths I have witnessed in my forty-five-year career as a nurse. It changed me, Fran. Her stories, and her words, touched me so deeply. But the way she died is beyond words. What a gift I was given having known her. Wait until I share with you how she passed away."

"Not to be rude, Jacks, but I want to change the subject. I've been approached by Dynamics Ltd. They want to buy my company. They've made me an offer I think I am going to accept. I'm selling my company. It's not for the money. As you know, I have more than I can ever spend, and I have no one to leave it to. I want to travel. I've been all over the world and explored none of it. I was in Rome and saw nothing but the inside of offices and hotel rooms. I went to every province, every State, and almost every country in Europe. I've been to China, South Korea, and even Russia. I did not visit anywhere. Now I want to be a tourist and visit the world while my health is good. I want to rent a Villa in Tuscany for a year and drink wine, and I want you to come with me."

"I'm floored, Fran. It all sounds great. I would love to someday do something like that. It just can't be now. I just signed a three-year contract with Sunset Haven Homes. I planned on retiring then. I can plan something with you after that if you like. I would love to travel. I have my heart set on a European river cruise."

"Come with me, and we'll do all the cruises you want. I will buy out your contract, and we can go as soon as six months. We've been friends forever, and I want to share the rest of my life with you. Two old maids on the loose in the world. It would be great. We both worked hard all of our lives, and we deserve to share it with someone like us…together. Jacks, you're all I have of family and friends. Let's share it together. Say that you will. At least say that you'll think about it."

"It's quite an offer, Fran. I have to admit that I am tempted to say yes right away, but I do have to think about it. You think about what you said also. That company is your baby. It's been your all for so long. Are you sure about this? And, why a villa in Tuscany?"

"I can travel to most of the places which interest me in Europe from there. It's a start. It would give me a home base. Give us a home base to visit Italy and neighboring countries, and then we could stay a year or six months elsewhere or just go by the seat of our pants. I don't want to do this alone, Jackie. I won't have the responsibilities of my business anymore, and I will have to face my own company and my loneliness. I've always been afraid of my feelings, and loneliness is the biggest of those fears. I've worked too hard to have it all end in loneliness. I really need you."

I didn't know what to say. Fran had never asked anything of me before, that I couldn't say yes right away. I had to think about this one. With what I now knew and the possible outcome of this weekend could very well take that generous offer away.

"Come on, let's go back home. I have a craving for potato chips after I eat ice cream."

"You'll never change, Jacks. Your eating habits have always been weird. Do you still eat muffins or cookies with your soup? I'll never forget the time we were at the Keg restaurant in St Catherine, and you asked for a piece of chocolate cake instead of crackers with your soup. The waiter was speechless, but he brought you what you wanted. I had tears falling in my soup, and I was laughing so hard. Everyone was looking at us to see what was so funny."

"I remember. He had the nerve to ask me if I wanted the crackers for dessert with my coffee."

"Would you like more wine with your chips? I just poured myself one."

"Fran, do you think about the past much? Home, school and the people you've met? Since I met Noula, I find myself in my past a lot, and I am trying to see things with a more mature attitude and an open heart. I've forgiven my father for drinking himself to death, and I've accepted my past. The things that were done to me and the terrible things I did. I was angry for so long. Noula showed me the way out of some of that anger and pain. She knew what they felt like"

We took our wine and chips out on the deck. It was a beautiful September night with the stars out in full sparkle and the moon reflecting over the ocean. The waves were barely a whisper. We sat in the quiet for a while, totally relaxing and enjoying the moment. I broke the silence when I resumed my story. Time was fleeting, and as Noula said, words were important.

"The next day, I took my entire afternoon off to be with Noula. I told her that I wanted to know more about her and her life. I knew that she was starting to fail. Her color was high all the time, and her lips and fingernails were getting a light blue tinge. I knew that we were running out of time."

"My brother, Paul and Eve, tried to have a child. Eve got pregnant twice and lost them both. Depression set in after the second miscarriage, and they both started numbing themselves with alcohol. I was scared for them. Their marriage was suffering as much as they were. Then God stepped in. One of the partners at the office, Alan DiFior, was approached by a friend who happened to work at an adoption agency in Moncton, New Brunswick. She asked him if he knew of anyone who was looking for a baby, a little girl. She did not want the baby to go through the system due to complications that it would create between agencies across provinces, and the only one who would suffer was the baby. There was a special request that came with this baby that it comes to Cape Breton, which Alan's friends wanted to honor. That was all the information she could divulge at that time.

Alan dropped that responsibility on my desk. He told me to make some inquiries and help him find a proper home for this baby. I said a prayer right away. I knew that there was a God and that he had answered prayers for a couple of friends I knew. What could I lose, right? I had such peace about the whole thing. I picked up the phone and called Paul. I told him to come to the office tomorrow at one with Eve. I also told him why and to make sure that they were sober and presentable.

Paul and Eve showed up at quarter to one. They looked great, better than I had seen them look in a long while. I had arranged with Mr. DiFior to meet with them and told him how much they wanted a baby. Alan called us into his office a ten past. He asked a lot of questions, which Paul and Eve answered correctly. He asked me about my personal involvement. I told him that Paul was my brother and a good man. He gave them papers to fill and gave me a non-conflict of interest and a non disclosure contract to sign as well.

He showed us pictures of the baby. She was so tiny and beautiful. Eve kept wiping her tears. Paul was visibly shaking. It was very emotional as well. Alan said that he would get back to us by Friday. He told me to stop my search for now until we get an answer from his friend in Moncton.

The answer came before Friday. It was Thursday morning when Alan told me to call my brother and Eve in to see him that afternoon. There was no indication of anything on Alan's face. I called my brother and told him to come in because Mr. DiFior wanted to see them. I also told him not to raise his hopes until we knew for sure. Mr. DiFior had not given me a sign either way. When they arrived, Alan called them into his office and told me to wait at my desk for an important call. I saw how nervous they both were. I felt kind of put out, but I did have a job to do, and he was my boss, after all.

Half an hour after Paul and Eve were with Alan, a woman walked in with a baby in a carrier car seat. She asked for Mr. DiFior. Alan came out as soon as I buzzed him. He then told me to wait with my brother in his office. I knew then that the baby was all ours. A few minutes passed, and the baby was handed to Eve. I had never seen my brother happier. Alan asked for the baby's name. They both said Maggie at the same time. Maggie Marie Fortier. I even had tears rolling off my face. Alan beamed with pride at his involvement in this precious event and choked back tears as he said," Welcome to your new family, Maggie Marie Fortier."

Life went on as usual. They were good parents and so very happy. They stopped drinking and did everything they could to make sure that Maggie was well cared for and wanted for nothing. Maggie was so bright, and her smile would stop traffic. They were a family at last. Eve quit her job at the restaurant and stayed home with Maggie. Paul, on the other hand, worked all the overtime he could get to make sure that his family wanted for nothing. Maggie started walking at eleven months, and her first word was not Mama or Papa; it was Jou-Jou. The dog's name was Bijou, and she called it Jou-Jou. We laughed so hard at that. She just kept saying Jou-jou with every outburst.

Tragically, Paul and Eve died in a car accident on their way home from the mall. They hit black ice, and the car went off the bridge and into the water. Maggie was three at the time. I was her godmother, so she came to live with me. Eve's family wanted nothing to do with the child seeing as she was not blood. I never told Maggie. I wanted her to know that she was chosen and special, and loved. I could not have loved her more if she were blood.

I took two weeks off work to bury Paul and close his estate. Eve's body was sent to her family, and they took care of things at their end. After probate, I never heard from them again. I found a sitter for Maggie. I wanted a reliable woman to come to my house. I did not want a repeat of what I had gone through. After interviewing four women for the position, I chose Bridget Hamilton. She lived nearby and had a little girl the same age as Maggie. She would bring her daughter to my house and watch the girls there. She was better than great. I was lucky enough to keep Bridget full-time until Maggie was in School. Bridget agreed to pick up Maggie at the bus stop along with her daughter and take Maggie to her place, where I would pick her up after work. It was perfect. Bridget was in our lives until Maggie was in high school.

I did not tell Maggie about her parents and how she got to be in our lives until she was sixteen. I wanted her to be at an age where she could understand without too much trauma. I told her that she had been chosen by my brother and Eve to be their daughter and that I was the proudest aunt. She took it well. We did a lot of crying and talking. She still called me Mother. Every now and again, she called me mom. We were very close.

She did well at school. She got interested in art and music. She was unbelievably gifted and sang like a bird. I bought her a stereo, headphones, and a piano, along with a tambourine. Anything she wanted or needed to develop her talents.

She was also an artist. See the painting over my bed? She did that for me for my fortieth birthday. I have it engraved in my memory. I see it all the time. It brings beauty in my darkness. I touch it sometimes to see it more clearly in my mind."

"Are you feeling tired, Noula? Do you need a break? I can get us some coffee if you like?"

"I would like to rest for a while. Not for very long. Can you give me an hour and then come back? Please, Jackie, will you come back?

"I took her hand in mine and assured her that I would be back in an hour."

"I took myself out for a muffin and coffee at The Charter. I had a lot to mull over. I was glad that I had taken the time to be with her and listen to her stories. She was opening her life to me so I would remember her. We definitely had some experiences in common. I believe that, somehow, she felt that. I, too, had lost a parent at a young age, as she had. My father died of alcoholism before the age of fifty. I was fourteen years old at the time, remember? Like Sally, in Noula's first story, I was alone, and my mother was absent too because she worked two jobs and kept borders. She did not want to go on welfare or have strangers raising me. She would get up at five every morning to make breakfast for the boarders and pack them a lunch; then she would do the washing and plan supper before going to clean at the church and then at the Grayson home twice a week. In between jobs, she would walk about a mile to get groceries and supplies at the Sobeys uptown, then walk back carrying those heavy bags a couple of times a week. Her hands would have cut across the knuckles from those bags sometimes. I would go with her when I was not in school and help lighten the load. That was basically the only help I was. I was at a rebellious age, and I was angry. I didn't make it easier on my mother. I never forgave her for not protecting me from George, the perverted neighbor. Fran, you and I were both touched by his perversion. We stayed clear of him even though he was no threat after your father got piss drunk and beat him within an inch of his life. Still, the damage was done, and we've been carrying that with us all these years. For me, the molestation has left me frigid and untouchable. But you, Fran, you went the opposite way. You became promiscuous but emotionally detached. You could give your body but never your heart, except that once.

I, too, had made friends with a kitten. Do you remember the feral kitten? I would sneak food out and put it under the porch for it whenever I could. It took a while for the kitten to come close to me and trust me. I will always remember the day it let me pet it. My little heart just welled with pride. Two weeks later, I found the kitten dead behind the shed. It had been poisoned. I still cry for that poor creature. Just like Sally, just like Noula."

"Jacks, why would you say I was promiscuous? Are you trying to make me feel bad? I know how difficult our past was. I don't want to go back there. Not for a minute do I want to revisit it? What's done is done. I've moved on. So why are you trying to take me back there?"

"I'm not taking you anywhere but on this journey through my experience with Noula. I need you to listen and not jump to any conclusions. I told you that I was thinking about my past but don't forget, and you were a part of that past. It makes sense that I would be thinking of you as well. Please, Fran, I need this."

"Ok, Jacks. I think I understand. I'm sorry."

"When I got back an hour later, Noula was sitting in her rocking chair talking with the doctor. He filled me in on her condition when I followed him out in the hall. Her oxygen levels were so low that he wanted to put her on portable oxygen, but Noula refused. He was hoping that I could convince her. I assured him that I would try but doubted that she would accept. I knew that Noula was ready to die and would not want to be dependent on any external help to prolong her life."

"The doctor does not understand my refusal of oxygen. I do not want anything to interfere with what God has planned for me. I do not believe in prolonging a life that has been lived to the fullest of its usefulness. I am ready to go home. Please sit with me some more. I have things which need to be said before I go. Not only important to myself but to whomever you share this with. They will own my stories as well."

"I knew then that she wanted me to know her stories so that I could share them with her granddaughter. I sat in the chair that the doctor had vacated. I asked Noula if she wanted me to call anyone. She simply shook her head no and resumed her storytelling."

"Maggie got a full scholarship to Ryerson in Toronto. That was how good an artist she was. She could have had a job as a graphic designer for some of the largest companies in fashion and corporate. She chose instead to work towards having her own show at Markson Art Studio in Quebec City. The biggest and most well-known art gallery in Canada. She had been invited by Mr. Markson himself after he had visited the university and saw her work. She had worked hard and long on an impressive portfolio to show him when she heard that he was coming. She was even invited to Quebec for a month to work under Mr. Markson. That was where she met Ronald Tanguay, Ronnie. He was from down-home, working as a master carpenter who specialized in unique framing. He had been hired by Markson to redo all the trim in his studio and make special adjustable frames.

It got serious really fast between Maggie and Ronnie. They had dated for a short time when Maggie got pregnant. Ronnie wanted to get married right away. He was so happy about the whole situation. Maggie was reluctant. She was so close to having her own show at the gallery. A baby would delay her dream. Nonetheless, she accepted her responsibilities to the baby and to Ronnie. They would get married right away.

She had a sit-down with Mr. Markson, and explained to him that she was pregnant and that she and Ronnie were going to get married, and that she would have to put her show on the back burner for now. He proposed to her that she at least put some of her paintings for sale in his gallery until she could accumulate enough work for her own showing. She was thrilled.

They got married in Old Quebec City and spent a week on an all-paid honeymoon, compliments of Mr. Markson. When they got back home to Cape Breton as Mr. And Mrs. Tanguay, we had a big party waiting for them. Ronnie had a big family, and the family was well-known in Richmond County. It was just me and a couple of old friends on Maggie's side. I had never seen her so radiantly happy.

They had a beautiful baby girl, Angel. They were so happy and proud. Maggie did a portrait of Angel. Angel and Ronnie, Angel and the puppy. She was consumed with motherhood. Ronnie built them a beautiful big house with a spectacular view of the ocean. It was awe-inspiring. Maggie started painting her surroundings. Her paintings were even better than the ones which had caught Markson's attention. She was so gifted.

Ronnie had made a wall in their basement with floor-to-ceiling windows overlooking the water and the rugged coastline. The view alone would have made an artist of anyone. While Angel was at school and Ronnie at his carpentry shop in the village, Maggie was painting in her studio for hours every day. They had a good life and a great marriage.

When Angel was ten, Maggie started losing weight, and her energy was low. She would go days without painting. She had no appetite. The doctor sent her for all kinds of tests, but they were inconclusive. I lived close by, in Arichat, and my hours at work were flexible, so I could help and be there for Maggie. I ended up leaving my job when Maggie was finally diagnosed with a rare form of lung cancer. They caught it too late. There was nothing that could be done to even try to prolong her life.

Before leaving the office, I went into Maggie's file, which had been transferred along with me to the Arichat office, to see if there was information about her parents which might help us. I was grasping at straws. Sometimes genetic and health history information is in the dossier. So, I just took the file with me without permission and left. I didn't look at it right away. When I got home, I sat myself down in the living room with a glass of cognac and opened the file I had brought with me."

Maggie was sent to Halifax for a battery of specialized tests. They were there for two weeks while I stayed behind with Angel. All results were the same. Nothing could be done. There was my Maggie, who had never smoked, dying of lung cancer. The oncologist in Halifax surmised that Maggie had been exposed to high levels of radiation for a long period of time, which triggered her lung cancer. The radiation was from radon gas. We all got tested, and we were all fine. Tests were done in our homes and places we lived before. We never found where she had been exposed.

When we got the news, I totally forgot about the file. We didn't need its information anymore. Though Maggie was very ill and the radiation was eating away at her bones, by some miracle, she was not in any pain. Maggie would console us. She was such a beautiful person.

One of my favorite things to do when I wanted to pray was find an open church. It so happened that the church in Arichat is open every day from dawn til dusk. When I found out about the church, I went there to pray every day. I would go when there was no one there. The doors were open until 8 pm every day, which made it easy for me to go. I felt peaceful in the church. It was easy praying in such tranquility. I had a lot on my mind and a lot to pray for. Maggie's health was number one for sure. It was also around the same time I was starting to have trouble with my sight, so I prayed for that as well. There was a homeless man who would sit near the small door at the top of the steps. He was there almost every time I went, so I even started praying for him. It came to a point where I would bring him something to eat every time I went to pray. He never asked for anything and was very polite and grateful for the food. There was something about him that made it easy to like him.

I prayed! Boy, did I pray? I cried, pleaded, and made deals with God. I would pray for hours. One day I found that I was not alone in the church. When I opened my eyes, I saw a man kneeling in the row of pews next to me across the aisle. We just smiled at each other and did not speak. This went on for a couple of days. The man and me, alone in the church praying. Then it happened. The man came across the aisle to where I was sitting and spoke to me. He said that his name was Raphael, no last name and that he had noticed how persistent I was in my hope to hear from God. He did not ask me any questions. He then said to me, "If God said to you that He would answer only one of your prayers, what would you pray for?" Then he put his hand up before I could answer him and said, "Say nothing now; think about it until Sunday afternoon and then ask Him."

I thought to myself that this man is a quack. He never even asked for my name or anything. When I got up to leave, he put his hand on my shoulder. For some unknown reason, I didn't feel threatened. On the contrary, I felt peaceful. I said to myself, "he must be a priest or a healer,"

I had heard of people like that. I looked him in the eyes and saw such compassion. So, I said that I would think about it, then I left. It was Friday afternoon, and he said that I had until Sunday afternoon to think about one prayer and only one.

"Jackie, I would like to lie down now. Can we resume this evening after meds?"

"I saw that her color was really off. I asked Noula if she needed anything or wanted to see the doctor. I told her that her color concerned me. She said that she just needed a rest. So, I left and went to The Charter for a bite and a drink.

I tell you, Fran, I was feeling uncomfortable with where Noula was going. This God thing and church and prayers. I know that she had great faith and that these were her stories, and that she was dying. Those were her memories she was sharing with me. They were not an intervention or a trap to take my soul. That's how uncomfortable I was getting, and I couldn't back out. I knew that it had nothing to do with me, but it was hard sitting there just listening when all I wanted to do was get away.

When I got back to the home after meds, I saw that the doctor was leaving Noula's room. I went to see how she was and saw that she had been put on oxygen. The floor nurse had called the doctor when she saw Noula's color and how shallow her breathing was. I knew that it was just a matter of time now. As I turned to leave her room, Noula motioned for me to sit. She pulled her oxygen mask down and resumed her stories. You can't refuse a dying person in their last moments. So, I sat.

"The more I thought about the prayer, the more I wondered who Raphael was and why he would say that to me. I went to the church again the same day before the doors were locked. Raphael was in the same pew he always was. I went and sat next to him. I asked him if he was a priest. Though he looked nothing like one, but who knows these days? He said no, that he was not. I then asked him if he was a healer. He answered that only God could heal and only when asked with a pure heart in the name of Jesus. Then you have to believe. Then I said, "If you're not a priest, then what are you?" All he said was, "All will be revealed, then you will know." With that said, he got up and left.

"What did he look like, Noula?"

"He looked like he was in his mid to late thirties, with light brown skin like a middle easterner, a well-trimmed beard, and beautiful dark brown wavy hair. You know, hair that made us women jealous. He was wearing regular jeans and a white linen shirt, the kind they wear in India with no buttons. He had sandals on and an amulet hanging from a leather lace around his neck. The amulet was a pair of wings. Honestly, he reminded me of a hippy. He spoke softly and had the most peaceful dark brown eyes I have ever seen. When he smiled, I felt a warmth I cannot explain. I figured that he had to be a healer or a Master Buddhist or something along those lines. There was nothing threatening about him. I was quite comfortable in his presence.

When I got home, I concentrated on my prayer list. I always prayed every day for family, friends, myself, and any other needs or wants that came to mind. I've been a prayer warrior for many years. Now I had to pick one specific prayer. Only one. That was going to be extremely difficult given Maggie's condition, my eyesight, Angel, etc.

The list had more than one request. I couldn't ask God for guidance or wisdom because those would have been prayers. So, I decided to just praise God instead. I praised Him with a smile and tears of joy running down my face. I just praised Him. I fell asleep praising God, still kneeling hunched over my bed. When I woke up, it was past midnight. I felt such peace that all I could do was continue praising God. It was automatic. I praised Him aloud with tears streaming from my eyes. Maggie walked into the room, wondering what was going on. She looked so tired, yet she had a comforting smile on her face. I didn't say a word; I just got up from my knees and held her in my arms. There were no words that fit the moment. Then we both retired for the day.

I got up early the next day and went to the church. The homeless man was there as always. I had never really spoken more than a courtesy. "Hello, how are you?" That morning I asked him if he was hungry and if he would like to come with me to The Charter for breakfast. He declined my offer and rose to walk away. I stopped him, and I asked him his name, apologizing for never asking before. He turned and smiled at me and just said, 'Ray will do just fine,' turned and left. I went inside the church to praise God some more. I could not stop myself. There, in the silence of the church, the prayer came to me. I knew what to pray for.

"Jackie, I'm feeling tired. Can you come back tomorrow?"

"I left Noula's room shortly after nine pm. I felt drained and sad. Noula was running out of time. I didn't know how to help her or what I could do for her. So, I took myself for a drive to clear my head. I drove past the church where

Noula went to pray and where she met the homeless man a couple of years ago. I drove around Isle Madame, slowly going through Noula's words in my head. Then I got an idea. I was looking forward to seeing her early tomorrow morning to spring my idea on her.

When I finally got home, it was already eleven. I took a nice soak in the tub while sipping a warm glass of cognac. I was determined to sleep well to be refreshed tomorrow for what I had planned. I got to the nursing home just after eight the next morning. Noula was sitting in her rocking chair, still in her nightgown and without her oxygen. She looked rested, and her color wasn't as off. As I walked in, she said, "Jackie, you never asked me what I prayed for?"

"I just smiled and told her that I trusted that she would tell me in due time. She laughed out loud at that. She said that she was right to have picked me to own her stories. Those are the words she used. Own her stories. Then she got serious and said, "I will tell you now."

"When I knew what I was going to pray, I went to the church Sunday morning, before mass, in the hope of seeing Raphael. I got there before seven. The doors were unlocked. As I went to go in, I saw Ray walking towards the front, coming from beside the church on the graveyard side. I greeted him by name for the first time. He smiled and said good morning to me. I asked if he would join me inside the church; I wanted to know more about him. He just said, "There's nothing for me in there. I don't go where I don't belong." then turned and walked away. You Know, that was the last time I saw him.

I went inside the church and looked around in the hope of seeing Raphael. I wanted to tell him my decision was made and what my "one" prayer was going to be. I found myself alone in the silence. I went to my pew of choice and started my prayer. I prayed for Ray. For his salvation…for him to know God in his life and for God to set free from the bondage that he was living in."

"What!? You prayed for the homeless man instead of for Maggie or your sight? Noula! I'm sorry, but I really don't understand that! My outburst didn't seem to faze her. She smiled and continued to explain her decision as though I hadn't said anything."

"Jackie, are you familiar with what King David did when his baby boy was sick and near death? It's in the Bible. King David had fallen in love with a married woman. Her husband was a captain in his army. He sent Rebekah's husband to the front lines during battle, knowing that he would be killed. He then married Rebekah and had a child. The baby was weak and deathly ill. David went to the temple and prayed to God day and night for his son's life. The baby died. David rose from the temple floor, went home and put his best clothes on and praised God, and rejoiced. People thought that he was crazy with grief. But he was not. He had accepted God's decision to take his baby home. Look it up, Jackie. It's an interesting story."

"Why not pray for your sight, then?"

"I will explain to you why I prayed for Ray.

Are you familiar with the stories of the lost sheep or why they called Jesus a wine imbiber in the Bible? There was a shepherd who had one hundred sheep. He noticed that one was missing, so he left the ninety-nine behind and went looking for the lost one. When he found it, he was pleased. You see, the ninety-nine were safely grouped together, but the lost sheep was in danger of being killed. And as for when Jesus was accused of preferring the company of sinners, he simply answered, "It's not the well who need a doctor." This is all in the Bible.

You have to understand that Maggie loved God. She had accepted Jesus as her savior at ten years old. She was strong in her faith. God, in His mercy, took Maggie home peacefully, and Maggie was in no pain. As for my eyes, I have seen enough beauty to keep me entertained in my darkness for the rest of my days, and I am, after all, sixty-nine years old. I am looking forward to standing before my God and hearing him say, "Well done, my faithful servant." He has given me so much that it would have been selfish to ask for more. I hope you understand better why I prayed the way I did. A person's soul is more important than anything else, including my eyes. Jesus gave His life for our souls, our salvation. Ray's was lost. Think about how long eternity is. Where would you like to spend it? With or without God?"

"Did God answer your prayer?"

"I don't honestly know. I never saw Ray ever again. So, no, I don't really know, but that's not for me to question. The creation does not question the reasoning of the Creator's decisions."

"I had to leave her room, Fran. I was shaking so much that I was vibrating. I gave her some lame excuse and left. It was mid-afternoon by the time I found myself parked in front of that same church, it was not my intention to go there, but when I saw where I was, I decided to go inside.

It's not a rich church. You could tell that it was old. Historical really. There is a plaque outside stating as much.

As I made my way to the altar, I noticed that I wasn't alone. There was a man near the back on the left of me. I just nodded and smiled, then went and sat in a pew at the front. The first thing I noticed was the man standing next to my pew. I looked up and said hello. He greeted me with the same and asked if he could sit down. I moved over and gave him a lot of room. He turned to me and said, "Would you be so kind as to bring Noula-May here tomorrow at three?" I don't think stunned is a good enough word to express my shock. I looked him straight in the eyes and asked who he was and how he knew that I knew Noula. He must know I work at the home; I thought to myself or has he seen me there at some time. He held my gaze before speaking. His eyes were hypnotizing. He said that his name was Raphael and that he had met Noula here many times. Then he said, "It's a small village, isn't it." I figured that's how he knew of me. It still freaked me out, Fran.

I wanted some time to myself to think and to calm my nerves. So, I got up and politely said goodbye and told him that if Noula was up to it and that she wanted to come, I would definitely bring her. Then I left. I drove to the beach near the bridge, and believe it or not, I asked God to guide me through this delicate adventure. It felt right doing that. I stayed there for about twenty minutes and went back to Sunset Haven.

When I got to Noula's room, I apologized for the way I had left and sat in her rocking chair. I didn't tell her that I had gone to the church and met Raphael and that he wanted to see her at the church the next day. Noula asked for my hand, so I moved the chair closer to her bed and gave her my hand. She held it in both of hers and thanked me for coming back and for being the friend that she needed at this time. She also said that she understood what I must be going through. Then she started sharing, again.

"Maggie passed away at the General in Sydney on September nineteenth. She had been hospitalized five days prior. For her comfort, she needed to be on oxygen and an IV. She was the one who asked to go there. She was put in a very nice palliative care room. She didn't want her home to be tainted by her death.

We were all by her side. Angel was sitting on the bed, holding her mother's hand to her heart. Ronnie was quietly crying, and I was praising God. I knew she was peaceful and in no pain. I knew she was ready to go home and that God would greet her with open arms. It truly was a bittersweet moment. Her passing was so peaceful. She even had a smile on her face and a glow about her. What a gift it was to see. Angel laid her head on her mother's breast and sobbed.

We left Maggie in the care of the hospital. They check if organs are healthy enough for harvesting. It's a common practice in Nova Scotia, as you well know unless otherwise stated. Her body was released to us the next day. We were told that her eyes, along with her liver, were taken. Our Maggie gave someone their sight back, Jackie. How wonderful and poetic, really. She was interred in the cemetery in Arichat overlooking the ocean. We had a private service, family only.

My eyesight was getting weaker, and it was just a matter of months before the light would completely leave me. I became totally blind ten months after Maggie died. Though I was ready, so I thought, but it was difficult to accept. I felt so helpless. I started getting panic attacks. Ronnie allowed Angel to stay with me most nights. That helped me a lot. I also got home care to come two hours a day for my personal care, and she would also make my meals. That's when I decided to give up my apartment and go into an assisted living situation. There was a unit coming available within a couple of months, so I gave notice, and the unit was reserved for me. That's how I ended up here, and it looks like here is where I will die.

I am so very grateful for how everything happened. I see God's hand in my care and bringing me here where I met you, Jackie. Thank you for listening to my stories and being such a blessed friend.

When I found out that my heart was failing, I asked Ronnie and Angel to please stay away. I needed to have this short time alone, which I consider a gift to myself. It is important to me to finish what God guided me to do. It had to be done this way for the greater good. It will all become clear to you soon."

"Noula, I went to the church before coming back here. I was so upset with what you had shared. Praying for a total stranger instead of Maggie or yourself makes no sense to me. Even after you explained it somewhat, it still doesn't register; I don't get it.

Shortly after I walked into the church, I saw a man kneeling in the back pew. He looked deep in prayer. When he noticed me, he rose to his feet and started walking towards me. There was something so peaceful about him that I didn't feel afraid or uncomfortable. He had such a beautiful smile. He had jeans and a white linen shirt with an amulet at the end of a leather lace hanging from his neck. It was a pair of wings. As he approached me, he put out his hand to greet me. I extended mine in welcome. When our hands met, I felt safer than I have ever felt before in my entire life. Nothing else existed. It was Raphael. That is exactly how you described him. He called me by my full name, Jacqueline. It only struck me later to question how he knew who I was. We sat together in the first pew near the candle caddie. We didn't speak for a long moment then he said, "Jacqueline, would you bring Noula-May here tomorrow at three?" I said that I would ask you and, if possible, I would bring you to the church. Then he rose and said, "I will see you both tomorrow at three then." With that, he turned and walked away."

"Yes! We must go. I will be ready tomorrow. Yes, I am ready!"

"She had such a smile on her face I had not seen before. She glowed! She started praising God out loud. I got up from the chair and touched her shoulder, and said that I was looking forward to bringing her to see Raphael at the church. Why he couldn't come to the home instead puzzled me, but who was I to question what was happening? Then I left her room to make arrangements for the outing.

"Jacks, are you telling me all this for a reason other than just sharing an old woman's last moments? I have to tell you, Jacks; I'm not feeling too comfortable. Are you converted, and this is how it happened, and now you're out to convert me?"

"Fran, don't ask questions, and don't freak out. You promised that you would listen until the end of the story. You promised. It's been a long day, and I'm exhausted. Let's call it a day and resume tomorrow after breakfast. It's already after 3 am. You said that you trusted me, Fran. Please."

I wish I could say that I awoke refreshed. I felt like I was drugged and in a fog. I'm afraid that Fran is going to bolt on me. I saw the fear in her eyes last night. She has never been able to face things that bring the slightest discomfort to her senses. Mention God or feelings or the past, and she runs away. It was getting close to where it was getting personal. God, if you're listening, HELP!

"Good morning. You look how I feel. Did we drink too much yesterday? I haven't felt this done out in decades. Are you almost done with your Noula story? Where's the coffee?"

"I'm just making a pot. I want bacon and eggs; what about you?"

"Sounds good, but only after my coffee. I'm going to take a shower first while the coffee is brewing."

While Fran was in the shower, I decided that it would be a good idea to pray. I needed help, but most of all, I needed God to sit on Fran, so to speak, so that she didn't spook and run off. I waited until after breakfast to even bring up Noula's name. We were sitting in the den, which overlooks the ocean. It was a peaceful scene with the gulls laying on the sand sunning themselves and the waves lapping a welcome for the birds to come in, and Vivaldi softly playing on the Bose in the background. Even Fran looked relaxed.

"All right, finish your story."

"Everything was in place. I had the wheelchair-accessible van for the afternoon, and my schedule was cleared. We left the home at two-thirty to give us enough time to get out of the van and into the church. I then had to park the van away from the doors. When I got to the church, Noula was waiting for me where I had left her in the vestibule. As we were heading towards the altar, I noticed Raphael was walking behind us. I turned Noula around to face him, and to my shock…yes, shock, Noula put out her hand towards him and greeted him by saying how happy she was to see him. Not in a figure of speech, Fran, she could "see" him!

I didn't say a word. Not even hello. I was stunned into silence. He took Noula by the hands and helped her out of the wheelchair, and sat her next to him in the pew. The look on her face was radiant. He looked at her and smiled, then said, "Noula, how would you like to see the answer to your prayer?" No sooner did he say the words that a man came out from behind a door just to the left of us. Noula extended her hand to him, and Raphael introduced him. "Noula, do you remember Ray?"

He looked familiar to me as well, but I couldn't place him. Then the man spoke, all the while holding Noula's hand, and with tears just streaming off his face, he said, "I want to thank you for your prayer, Noula. You saved my life. I was a drunk, for over forty years, with no will to live or desire to change my ways. I stayed numb and was too much of a coward to end it and just kill myself, so I drank until my liver was going to do the killing for me. I was taken to the hospital, and against all odds, I got a new liver…a clean second chance. When I woke from the transplant, the doctor explained to me that I was the luckiest man he had ever known. Seeing as I was a drunk, there was no chance of ever being eligible for a new liver unless I was sober for over one year. God knew that wasn't going to happen because I was so lost and weak. The only way I could get a new liver was if the liver came from an immediate family member. I had no family, so I thought."

"Noula-May, Maggie was his family. She was Ray's biological daughter. You see Noula-May, God answered not only your single prayer. Look at all your prayer has done. Your one prayer has already touched many, and it will live on through those it has touched."

After Ray said those words and tearfully thanked her, Noula said in a whisper, "Thank you, my dear God, thank you." and then she laid her head on Raphael's shoulder. As he was holding Noula, I noticed that the amulet was shining so bright from his neck, a light I cannot explain; then I heard him say to Noula, "Well done Noula-May, now you can go home." with the words being said Noula passed away in his arms. He looked up at me and simply nodded his head. I took my cell phone out and called for the doctor to come to the church and pronounce Noula dead.

Raphael held her in his arms the entire time until the doctor and the stretcher came. Ray had left by then. It was the most heartwarming, life-changing moment of my life, Fran. After Noula's body was gone and it was only Raphael and me left in the church, I asked him if he was a priest. He answered by saying that he was one of many who serve God, then turned and walked away. I never saw him after that.

I went to the nursing home from the church. I had papers to fill out, and I had to try and get a number for Angel. When I got to the home, Jane, the nurse on duty, pulled me aside to my office. She showed me the box which Noula had left for me, along with her precious painting. Jane then told me that Noula had thanked everyone personally and said her goodbyes. That did not surprise me. Noula had a sense that she was going home that day.

After finishing the paperwork and calling Ronnie and Angel, I went home with the box Noula had left for me. I was too emotionally drained to look into the box right away, so I poured myself a glass of wine and stood the painting on the couch. It was of Nouls sitting in a meadow with a peacock half on her lap with his tail closed, caressing the side of her leg. She was looking up at the clouds with her hand on the peacock. In the clouds, I saw a little girl holding a kitten to her heart, a gannet in flight, and the head of a seal coming out of the cloud. I was mesmerized. There's the painting behind you on the wall. The entire day, the whole experience, was nothing less than a miracle, Fran. I always wanted to believe in God, but I never let myself do so. I was afraid I would become someone else. Someone like the people that turned me off of God. But I felt so different and so much at peace inside, even with the turmoil in my head. There was peace. So, I praised God out loud, raising my glass of wine towards heaven, and thanked him.

I then got up and got my laptop to look up King David and the death of his baby. I found the story in 2 Samuel:12. The more I read, the more I understood why Noula didn't use her one prayer for Maggie. I must have thought about that for over an hour before I then looked up Jesus and the sinners. I found that same story in Matthew 9-10:17 and in Mark 2;15-22 and again in Luke 5;29-39. It all started to make sense, and I really started to grasp the depth of Noula's wisdom. Then I looked up the parable of the lost sheep. All of a sudden, I saw Ray, the homeless man…the lost soul. Then I was a lost soul. Fran, I'm not lost anymore. And Fran, I now know who Ray is and why he looked so familiar.

Remember when I told you that on my last week, there was a bum brought in by ambulance, and he struck me as familiar? Then again, I was struck that day he met and thanked Noula. Fran."

"STOP right there! I don't want to hear anymore! My heart is pounding in my ears, and I've trouble breathing. Don't say anymore. Jackie, I'm afraid of what you will say next. You know better than to trap me in this kind of situation!

"Fran, the truth cannot hurt you. This cannot hurt you. You do need to hear what I have to say. You promised. At least let me tell you what Noula left for me in the box.

After I closed my laptop, I poured myself another glass of wine and emptied the box on the coffee table. There were two photo albums, which I didn't open right away, a letter addressed to me and another letter folded in a yellowed envelope. I also found a charm. It was identical to the wings on Raphael's amulet. I held it to my heart and sobbed.

I read the letter that Noula had typed for me. It was beautiful. She thanked me for being her friend and that she trusted me to do the right thing with her stories. You see, Fran, that's why I called you here this weekend…to do the right thing with Noula's stories. I had to share them, and in my heart, it had to be with you. I want you to read the letter which was in the yellowed envelope."

I could see the signs of fight or flight in Fran's eyes. Her face was stone, and her hands were visibly shaking. My own heart was pounding in my ears as well, and I swear I could hear my blood passing by my eardrums. Fran took the letter and held it in her hands for a while before opening it. I looked at Fran, and in a whisper, I just said, "Please." She then read the letter.

To Whom it may concern;

This letter is a plea from my heart. Please, I beg of you, please honor my request. My name is Constance Demers, and I am the natural grandmother of the baby girl who was born May 30th, 1978, to Francine Ester Poulin at the Moncton General Hospital. The baby's father is my son, Raymond Joseph Demers.

I have no idea where my son is at the moment. He's been gone since he and Francine broke up. That is why I am making this request. Can the baby please be sent to Cape Breton for adoption? I know that one day this will be very important to the child and parents. I know in my heart that you will honor my request.

Forever grateful
Connie Demers

"Fran, Ray at the church is Raymond. I know that now. He didn't recognize me, just like I wasn't sure who he was. Fran, talk to me, please."

Fran rose to her feet, her entire body vibrating with emotion. She stood motionless, just shaking and silent for a while, and stared at the letter she had dropped on the floor.

Then she turned and looked me in the eye and screamed at the top of her lungs, "How dare you! You knew better than to do this to me! You're dead to me!" Then turned and stormed out. I wasn't surprised at all. I expect Fran to react this way. This is where my newfound faith should come in, I guess. I said a simple prayer putting the entire situation in God's hands. God knows Fran better than I do.

The next morning, I went to the church to talk to Raymond. I was actually excited. Raymond and I used to be good friends' way back when. We both loved and tolerated Fran. We knew how damaged she was, and we both wanted to protect and care for her. She was the love in Raymond's heart and the sister I never had. When I walked into the church, Raymond was in the vestibule, hanging the banner to announce the funeral in two days from now. Noula's funeral. I guess it was customary to hang the silk banner to let parishioners know so they could come to celebrate the life of the departed and pray.

I didn't plan on staying long, so we talked in the vestibule, standing near the big doors. The minute I spoke, he recognized me. He said that I had looked familiar to him yesterday, but he was so nervous about meeting Noula and emotional that he put the thought out of his head.

When he said, "You look good, Jacks." I had to reach out and touch him. No one else ever called me Jacks except Fran. I told him what a blessing it was to see him and that I wanted him to come to dinner tonight. It was very important that he come. I had so much to tell him and to show him as well. I gave him the piece of paper I had prepared with my address and phone number. He agreed and said he knew the place and would be there at six. I gave him a long hug and left.

I ordered dinner from the Charter. I was in no frame of mind to cook. Raymond arrived at five to six, dressed in a nice shirt and jeans. He had changed from his work uniform and showered. He walked in and gave me a kiss on the cheek, and said how nice it was that we were here together. I've always liked Raymond. He was always such a sensitive man.

It was small talk all through dinner. I had a glass of wine, and Raymond had coffee. He said that he didn't even crave alcohol anymore. He was free from that bondage. He told me that when he recovered from the surgery, he came back to Arichat, and that's when he met Raphael on the steps of the church. Raphael offered him a full-time position as a verger for the parish. We then talked about when we hung out together, the three of us. I was the tag-along. They never minded. When they wanted to be alone, they would just tell me, and I would make other plans or just stay home. We got into dances and bars while still too young to drink just so we could listen to the music and dance. Neither of us drank back then. We got caught skinny dipping in the public pool after hours at night more than once. We would climb the fence and swim for hours. We had a great time. We often got caught climbing out. We laughed so hard at our reminiscing that Raymond got the hick-ups. We laughed even harder. After dinner was over, we retired to the den for more serious talk.

"Why did you leave the way you did and not keep in touch, Raymond? When Fran told you that she was pregnant, you just ran."

"Is that what you think, Jacks? Is that what Fran told you? I was so happy about the baby. I knew we were young, but I also knew that I could take care of Fran and the baby. I was excited about being a father and a husband. When I told my mother that Fran was pregnant and that I was going to ask her to marry me, she offered us her blessing and told me that we could live in the rental she owned in D'Escousse. I went to Fran's loft to ask her to elope and I told her that we had a bigger place than her loft to move into before the baby arrived. She told me to go home and give her time and space to think about it. The next day Mom found a hand-delivered letter in the mailbox addressed to me. It was more of a note than a letter. It was from Fran. Here read it for yourself."

Raymond handed me a tattered letter that was falling apart on the folds. It looked so fragile that I refused to touch it and asked him to read it to me. He recited the letter. He knew every word by heart. All I saw was sadness in his eyes as he spoke these words:

"My dearest Raymond

I'm afraid that I have to say no to your proposal. I am not ready to be a wife and mother. It's not in my plans for my life. However, I do love you, just not enough to give up my dreams. Please do not try and find me or contact me if you do. I'm sorry that it has to end this way, but it has to.

I've gone out of province to take care of this. Alone! I wish you all the best in life.

Fran."

He sat there looking into space for a while. I didn't want to intrude on his thoughts, so I sat back and waited to speak. After giving him what I thought was enough time, I brought him back to the moment and asked him, "Raymond, what do you know about your daughter, Maggie?"

"I know that she saved my life, and I'm not just referring to the liver I now have. I don't know much more than that. They don't give out information about your donor, and the family of the donor doesn't know about the recipient. I was told it was my daughter's liver by mistake. They thought I knew my own daughter. I was a perfect match to her, which meant that she had to be my child. When I asked who she was, they said that they could not breach the confidentiality of the donor or her family. I just found out her name and met her mother at the church yesterday when Raphael told Noula that Maggie saved my life and that I was the man who received Maggie's liver when she passed away. Now it's too late to know my child or anything about her. She's gone, and so is her mother."

"Raymond, I want to tell you that you have a granddaughter. Her name is Angel, and she lives near here. I've not met her, but I have talked to her father, Ronnie, when Noula passed away. Would you like me to call him and make arrangements to have him meet us at the church tomorrow? And Raymond, I also have these."

I handed Raymond the photo albums and the letter that his mother had written to the adoption agency in Moncton when she had heard that the baby was born. I don't know how she found out, but apparently, she did.

Raymond read the letter first and put his head in his hands, and wept. I left the room to give him some privacy by excusing myself to make us some coffee. Alone in the kitchen, I, too, cried. Fran should have stayed here for this. I was hurting for both of them. It was all so tragic, yet in an inexplicable way, it was so right. It was as though the truth was finally freed from its bondage of sadness to heal the past.

When I came back with the coffee, Raymond was looking at the pictures in the album. It was the one that held the photos of Maggie as a baby all the way up to high school. Tears freely flowed from his eyes, and a sad smile revealed the pain in his heart. He looked up at me and said, "I've missed so much. She was so beautiful. She looked like Fran. I'm so grateful that she was loved."

"I have something else to tell you, Raymond. I know you're feeling overwhelmed with all of this, but there's more. Fran was here. She came down Friday for the weekend. I had invited her to come so that I could tell her about Noula and Maggie, along with everything else. She listened to what I had to share but bolted like a deer in headlights when it got too emotional. After she read your mother's letter, she lost it. I've never seen her so shaken. I haven't heard from her since she left late Sunday afternoon."

"I really don't know how to feel right now, Jacks. So much to take in. Overwhelmed doesn't come close to expressing how torn up I feel inside. I now know that God is with me, but this seems bigger than he is at the moment.

I have mourned the loss of Fran and my baby for over forty years. I lived in a bottle with my self-pity to keep me thirsty. I feel angry, I feel cheated, yet I also feel grateful and blessed. I have forgiven Fran, but I haven't quite got the hang of forgiving myself. I have no one but me to blame for my wasted life."

Raymond left early enough for me to call Ronnie to ask him to meet me at the church tomorrow morning after Angel left for school. Noula's celebration of life was to be the day after, and I needed to see him before that. He agreed with no hesitation.

When I got to the church the next morning, Raymond was replacing the burnt candles at the front of the church. He gave me a sheepish smile and finished what he was doing. Ronnie arrived at nine. He looked tired. He walked over and introduced himself, and we shook hands. I properly introduced myself, seeing as we had only spoken on the phone twice. I then called Raymond over and introduced him. We sat in the front pew, and I started with the reason I had asked him there.

"Ronnie, Raymond is the man who received Maggie's liver. He is also Maggie's biological father. That's how he got the transplant; otherwise, he would have been refused, and they would have let him die because he was not eligible due to the fact that he had a drinking problem. Maggie was the only one who could have saved him."

Ronnie was speechless for a long while. He would look from Raymond to me. It wasn't hard to see how difficult this moment was for him. We all three sat down then Ronnie spoke.

"Maggie wondered if you were still alive. She would have loved to meet you. We have a daughter of our own; Angel is her name. Maggie had your eyes. Would you like to meet your granddaughter?"

"Thank you for meeting us here today and for sharing that Maggie had my eyes. That means so much to me, and yes, I would be so honored to meet Angel, my granddaughter, but only if she wants to. I would totally understand her not wanting to meet the man who abandoned her mother."

Raymond did not try to hide his tears. They were flowing freely from his eyes. Ronnie got up from his pew and walked across the aisle to where Raymond was sitting, and offered him his hand. He told Raymond that he would speak to Angel and absolutely leave it up to her if she wanted to meet him. Then he said his goodbyes and left. Just before going out the door, he turned and asked if we would be in attendance at Noula's funeral. We both shook our heads, yes.

Minutes after Ronnie left, the door opened again. I thought that it was Ronnie coming back for some reason. As soon as I realized it wasn't Ronnie but Fran, Raymond had already spoken her name. They both stared at each other for what seemed forever then Fran broke the silence.

"I saw your car outside, Jacks, and figured you would be in here. I went to your place first. Jacks, I'm so sorry for the way I acted and the way I left. My behavior was totally unacceptable. Please forgive me. The only way I could function all my life was if I forgot the past. It was easier to avoid and seem heartless than to feel the hurt, the rage, the loss, and face the fact that nothing could ever change all that has happened to me. I admit that some of it was my fault, but I was young and damaged. I acted the only way I knew how to survive. I can't run from myself or my past anymore. I learned that on the weekend.

Raymond, I'm so very sorry. I lost my heart to you and never found it again. Fear stopped me from loving anyone the way that I loved you. Now I doubt that I even have a heart. I have not felt my life. My loss, my decisions. I ignored all my feelings and walked away from a life I couldn't face. Leaving was my way of claiming my life, and I did claim it. No one ever got close enough to hurt me physically or emotionally. The only person from my past I kept contact with was you, Jacks. I didn't make it easy on you with all my restrictions and controls. But you stayed my friend no matter how I treated you. Why?"

"You're all I kept in my life from my past as well. I love you like a sister. We were both harmed by our past. We did the best we could. I don't regret my life, Fran. I lived it my way, as did you. Noula prayed for me to find peace and the love of God. I couldn't resist her prayers anymore. She showed me that God is real, and I see that now. Finding him this late in my life made the journey worth every step. I'm at peace and free from the anger and the hatred that ate away at me my entire life."

I looked at Raymond and saw that he was like a statue bolted to the floor. There was no readable expression on his face. Fran was the one to walk towards him. The closer Fran got I could see that Raymond was visibly shaking. Fran said his name and collapsed on the floor, sobbing. Raymond closed the distance and put his hand on her shoulder.

"Fran, I blamed you for a long time for the failure I became in my life. It was easier to blame you than to face the fact that I was a coward hiding in a bottomless bottle. We were so young. I didn't have a dream or a vision for the future. You did. My world back then was me and then you.

I've taken responsibility for what became of me. For the first time in my life, I feel like a man, a free man. I know what it is to waste one's life. For me, that stopped when I received a second chance. I plan on living to my very best with the man I have become. I let you down and myself too, and didn't take my head out of the bottle long enough to see past the bondage of my own making. I am so thankful today for all that God has given me."

And with those words said, Raymond extended his hand to Fran and helped her to her feet, then he held her in an embrace. They both cried away their personal pain and let go of the hurt that had defined them for all those years. For Raymond, it was a celebration of freedom from self-pity, and for Fran, well, for the first time in over fifty years, Fran faced her fear of feelings and opened her heart to the love of God.

"Fran, Angel, your granddaughter, will be here tomorrow for Noula's funeral mass. Will you come with me and Raymond? Ronnie, her father, is telling her about you and Raymond."

"I would love to meet her. I admit that terrifies me. It's been a long time since I have allowed myself to feel anything. That changes today. I also believe that this is my second chance. I'm really not the type to make the same mistake twice. The first one cost me way too much. Raymond, I'm so sorry for leaving the way that I did when I got pregnant. I didn't give you any consideration. I see how hurtful that was, and I am so very sorry."

Fran, Raymond, and I walked in just minutes before Noula's casket was brought in. There was Ronnie's family sitting to one side in the front and along with some local mourners scattered throughout the church, who attended most funerals. Then there were the three of us. As Noula's casket rolled by us, Ronnie stopped with Angel at his side and extended his hand to Fran, and motioned Raymond and me to follow. Angel reached out and took them both by the hand. Fran on her right and Raymond on her left. I walked alongside Ronnie. There wasn't a dry eye among us as we all walked in honor to the front. After the funeral mass, Noula was laid to rest next to Maggie in the cemetery with a view. It was a beautiful goodbye.

Fran was true to her word. She allowed herself to feel everything. I've never seen her so sensitive. She opened up like never before. She even cried at a cartoon about a big dog who loved a kitten that was on TV, which she was watching while I was fixing dinner for us when she had come down to pick up Angel for their trip to France to visit the Louvre, then to Italy. They were leaving the next morning bright and early. It had been Maggie's dream to one day visit France and Italy to experience the art and culture.

Fran was a new person. She enjoyed being a grandmother, and she was good at it. Ronnie was happy for Angel that she was close to her new grandparents. Raymond was just as involved. Fran and Raymond remain good friends to this day. When Fran comes down to my place, Raymond will come over for a meal and sometimes stay to play Scrabble with us. It all feels so normal and familiar. We never saw Raphael again, but we all three of us believe that he was one of God's Archangels.

As for me, after Fran sold her company, she bought out the remainder of my contract at Sunset Haven. I am now retired and free to travel. She booked us on a river cruise. The longest river cruise we could find in Europe. We leave in a month with no return date. Our lives are better than we could ever dream. All I can say for that is, "Praise God for Noula's Prayer!"

The House That Called Me Home

"It would be a summer getaway for me! Just a summer vacation home… "

A summer home? There was that dream again. This was at least the third time I had had a similar dream. It was a dream about me buying a vacation home in the village where I was born. It always left me feeling like I was being called to my birthplace. It wasn't a nagging of sorts but more of an "okay, I'll look into it" kind of reaction.

This idea of owning a property in Quebec was not a new one. I would often search the web pages for properties for sale but in Percé, Quebec. My heart felt at home there for some reason. I stopped questioning that four trips ago. I accept the fact that my birth province of Quebec, along with my heritage, would always be a longing for me. It's in my genes and DNA. I just found it odd that my village, near the base of the Appalachian Mountains, was playing on my mind, in my dreams, and now during my day. This had only been a point of conversation before this, never more than that for me.

I left my village of St. Magloire, Quebec, by no choice of my own when I was a mere two-year-old toddler. My parents sold their house after my maternal grandfather, Joseph Mercier, passed away. Our parents packed us up and moved us to Ontario. My brother, Richard, who is three years older than me, has a few memories of where we came from, but he admits that the memories have faded to near nothing. He does, however, remember our grandfather dying in the downstairs bedroom and then his body being all dressed up, lying on the kitchen table with people coming and going all day and evening for two days. It was an old-fashioned wake. He also remembers the absence of crying over the old man's death. He says that he can still see our mother petting her father's forehead and face while sobbing over him after everyone had left. The only tears for the old man.

We had heard stories about our grandfather, Joseph, and how mean and hateful he could be towards his daughters. The only son he had fathered died at childbirth along with his wife, our maternal grandmother. He became a secret drinker and just got meaner and drunker as the years went on. My mother was the only one of five girls who stayed at home. She hadn't left her father alone like the other four siblings had. She honored him and stayed behind to care for him until his death. His cold heart finally stopped beating in 1956.

***

I had never been happy in Ontario. The place held too much unforgivable history. Though this place afforded me a successful career, it never held my heart. I finally escaped the Niagara Peninsula 13 years ago, a year after my husband, Samuel Drake, passed away. I use the word escape because that's what it felt like, and it took serving a life sentence of over forty-five years to get out. I am now very happy and very free living in the Cape Breton Highlands, where I feel God's presence in the vastness and beauty of his hand's creations. Though I live alone, I am never lonely.

After having the dream, the first time, I went looking on the website of St Magloire to check out what it had to offer, and I even looked at properties for sale. This is not uncommon for me. I often look at properties all over the country in all ten provinces. I do that for fun and to pass the time away.

Nothing looked familiar to me. I had only been back to St. Magloire in 1960, a year after the death of my father, and again in 1973, while on a short vacation. It was more or less just a drive-through, considering we only stayed an hour or so. I did, however, get to see the house that I was born in, though I doubt I could ever find it again on my own.

Seeing as we lived too far from hospitals and back in 1954, it was easier to give birth at home than drive a couple of hours to a decent hospital. Both my brother and I were born in that same house. Oh yeah, I was there again two years ago. How could I forget? I got to see the street that the house was on but didn't remember which house it was. While I was there, I had purchased a book about my mother's seven cousins who were famous strong men. All seven of them were world-famous and still to this day. Two of them still hold undefeated records of feats of strength to this day. Paul, the strongest, became a professional wrestler.

I'm not getting anything done today. I can't seem to have much control over my mind. It wants to stay in the dream and ride the feelings which it evokes. Might as well humor it and look at real estate in the village.

***

After spending two hours reading all I could find on the internet about St Magloire, my family name, real estate properties for sale in the area, and accommodations, I decided to start planning a vacation for a week or so and explore my birthplace and the nearby villages. Who knows, I might find that I still have relatives there or near there in neighboring towns. I could likely get away from my routine and social obligations in mid-May. This would give the spring thaw a good start. Though I'm sure there would still be some snow in the mountains and villages at least until June, if not longer. Quebec is known for its winter snow. It's like it has a competition within its borders to see where the snowfall would break the previous year's accumulation record. The mountain areas always won.

After sharing all this with my best friend, Patty, about my dreams and the feelings they left behind, I couldn't help but wonder if, in fact, it would be a good idea to own a little property in St Magloire. It felt right for some reason. I could use it to spend time in my birthplace and explore my family's history, and to get a fuller essence of who I am and my make-up, so to speak. Explore my roots. Patty expressed that she would love to be with me on the initial trip to help me find a place. She sounded more excited than me about the prospect of an adventure that this recurrent dream created. She jumped at the chance of a vacation together.

***

Patty and I decided to meet in Percé and drive to St. Magloire together from there. I would drive up from Nova Scotia and pick her up at the Gaspe airport. This would add another two and a half days on the road. We always wanted to experience Percé together, but time was never on our side. Now that I'm completely retired, and Patty can use her vacation time for personal trips, seeing as her kids were grown and gone, we could finally make it happen.

***

I picked up Patty at the airport early afternoon the day after I had arrived in Perce. We were staying overnight in the same cabin I had been renting every time I visited this place. We ate out at the nicest restaurant for lobster and brought a couple of bottles of wine and a bundle of firewood back to the cabin. It was a windless and warm evening with a full moon over the water and more stars than the sand on the beach. A gift of an evening, in good company, a nice wine to enjoy in front of a campfire with the waves from the Gulf of St Laurence filling our senses.

Next day we left Perce right after brunch for St. Magloire. We arrived in the village the same day, just past ten pm. I had found for us a B&B on the main street and requested a late check-in. It seemed to be the only accommodation in the area. This would be my first time in a B&B, but only because I could not find anything else. Not my accommodation of choice. Patty, on the other hand, loves them.

We walked the streets of the village, trying to get our legs to work again and get a feel of the place. It was a nice evening to do so. It was quiet out, and we seemed to be the only ones around. Even the only convenience store was closed. It had been a long day on the road, so we called it a day and went to bed.

***

After a good cup of coffee in our veins, we went for a walk in the village. Just outside the B&B was the church, which stood out larger than life right in the center of the village. It was a work of art and a true imbalance of wealth and power in an all too familiar scene found in small villages of Catholic communities. With a population of less than nine hundred people, the old church loomed over the village like the cathedral in Montreal. The cemetery was on both sides and along the back. Its population was much larger than the living one. As we walked the cemetery grounds looking for my relatives, I caught a glimpse of a "for sale by owner" sign on the street directly behind the church. I knew from previous trips that it was the street where I was born.

I felt a flutter inside as we neared the house where the sign was. It was almost like a premonition. Of what…I don't know, but it made my heart pound in my ears, and the spit leave my mouth. Patty asked me what was wrong.

Apparently, I had lost all color in my face, and my eyes mirrored the anxiety I felt inside. How silly!

I didn't want to look into that property today. Not with the way I was feeling, so we continued our walk around the village, just talking about nothing important. It was what I needed at the moment. There were two other properties for sale which were listed with a Realtor. I told Patty that I wanted to look into the private sale first and then maybe call the Realtor and set up a time to look at the others.

After lunch, we drove around the countryside. I found the old homestead where my mother was born by following the directions I received from the owner of the B&B. I had asked her if she knew where the Mercier farm used to be. We came upon the abandoned farm just before the next village's signage, just like she had said. No one had lived there since 1950 when my grandfather had moved in with my parents in the village. The barn had totally caved in on itself, and all that was left of the house was its foundation.

The day went by so fast that when we got back to the village, it was almost bedtime. We settled in our room right away and enjoyed a glass of wine before going to bed. It was a nice way to relax and talk about the adventures of our day. We were both tired from being hiking tourists. Tomorrow we will be house hunters.

I had a restless night with another one of those dreams about a house I was looking at in the village. In my dream, there was a stained-glass window above an old claw-footed bathtub. I couldn't make out the image, but the colors were of different shades of blue and green. It left me with a troubling but familiar feeling. The rest of the house was the same as in the other dreams. It seemed that every time I had a dream of the house, it revealed more of itself to me. I was more puzzled than ever.

After our morning coffee, laced with Bayleys, we made our way to the street behind the church to see if we could have a look at the house. I went up to the door alone. Patty stayed on the public sidewalk, slowly walking towards the neighboring homes. After just a few seconds, the door opened, and there stood an elderly woman holding a large black and white cat. I told her that I would like some information about the house and that I was in the market to purchase it. She said that we could come in and that she would be happy to answer all our questions over a cup of tea. I guess she saw us coming and knew that there were two of us. I called out to Patty to join us and waited for her to arrive at the door.

Once inside, the woman introduced herself as Estelle Garand. I introduced Patty and myself, leaving out my maiden name. The village would know me as Celine Drake and not Celine Thibault. I didn't want anyone to know that I was a Thibault from this village. Estelle made a pot of green tea and served us homemade molasses cookies. My favorite treat. That took me back to when my mother would make them for company. I would eat five or six before she would put them out of my reach and shoo me away.

I asked Estelle why she was selling. She told us that she was on a short list to get into the senior's home, the one just next to the cemetery. She was told that they would allow her in as soon as she sold her house. Estelle was 82 now and had come back to her roots when she was 60 and retired. She said that she purchased the house from Hector and Anne-Marie Menard. They had owned it for years and did a lot of upgrades to it. I asked her who the original owners were. She said that they were Xavier and Valerie Thibault. They had moved away many years ago. I went totally silent for a moment. I don't believe I even breathed. Patty looked at me as though to inquire as to what the hell I was doing. The silence in the room was getting uncomfortable, and Patty, not a French-speaking woman, couldn't even enter into a conversation to break the tension. Estelle just looked at me with a polite but confused smile on her face. When I composed myself enough to say something, I asked Estelle, with a crack in my voice, if she knew the original owners. She told me that she grew up right next door and knew them well but lost touch with them when they moved away to Ontario.

I asked how much she wanted for the house. She said that she would be happy with $25,000, furniture included. The money didn't really mean anything to her, seeing as she was alone in life and going into a nursing home. She would, however, like to sell the house to someone who would love it as much as she had. That's when we all got up and went about looking at the house and all it had to offer.

We had been sitting in the living room, which had an open concept to the kitchen and dining area. There was a combination bathroom/laundry room to the left of the back door, which led to a mud room and the backyard. There was Estelle's bedroom near the front entrance and a staircase from her bedroom to a full second-floor loft with a full bathroom. It was a large room with lots of light. It was filled with beautiful antique furnishings. Love at first sight. When I turned to look at the rest of the room, I gave out a gasp that startled both of them. I started coughing right away to deflect from my reaction, acting as though I had choked on my own spit. Patty knew that something was amiss. There it was, through the open door to the bathroom, my dream from last night...a stained-glass window above a claw-footed bathtub in the upstairs bathroom with a beautiful peacock in the center made with stained glass, with a cascading tail dawning all of its blues and greens. It looked like the peacock tattoo on my arm, which was well hidden under the sleeve of my shirt. Patty's uneasiness was visible. She, too, noticed the peacock. Estelle looked at her and then at me. I told Estelle that Patty was tired from our trip, and seeing as we hadn't slept well last night, it was affecting us.

We made plans to go back the next day to look at the rest of the house and outside the property. I had to get out of there quickly and put my brain back from my gut to my head. We walked in total silence until we got to the little café where we had been yesterday. I looked at Patty and said, "That's the house where I was born." She just nodded. I then said. "Holy shit...the peacock!" We then sat in silence again, not knowing what to say or think.

When we left the café, still not talking about the peacock, we agreed to go explore the neighboring villages. My father's family came from Armagh, just twenty minutes or so from St Magloire. I knew that I still had relatives there, cousins, who might recognize me from previous visits. We all look related, and we can spot a cousin from a distance. We hadn't been in Armagh for half an hour when I heard a woman call my name out loud. When I turned in the direction of the voice, I recognized my cousin Rachellle. We exchanged pleasantries for a few minutes, not saying why I was down, and then we parted ways. I didn't want to put Patty in an awkward situation with my cousin and me only conversing in French. Rachelle had to pick up her youngest child from daycare which made for a nice, polite breakaway.

We chose to have dinner at the hotel in Armagh. This establishment was built and operated by my uncle Roger Thibault for twenty-plus years until he sold it to the Gilbert family. They were cousins on my grandmother's side of my father's family. We shared some small talk during our meal which gave me a comfortable opening as I braved the subject that had been uncomfortably avoided. I started by going over the dreams I had had from the first to the one I had the night before last. They all had something different, leading to a reveal still to come. The one thing which unnerved me the most was the dream about the stained-glass window, with its blues and greens, and then seeing the peacock over the claw-footed bathtub in the bathroom upstairs.

I knew that Patty didn't much believe in psychic stuff, that is until she met me. I have a discerning gift, and the peacock window reaffirmed it. I could tell what people were thinking at times, and I felt things before they happened, so she was spooked more so than she was surprised at the current events. She said that she believed that I was being called to this place for reasons still unknown. She also believed that it would be a major event or a life-changing reveal. Seeing as I was being called to my birthplace, I totally agreed with her. While we were talking, I felt a surge of excitement at the prospect of what I might learn.

It was too late to call Estelle and confirm our viewing for tomorrow. Patty and I sat in our PJs, sipping a nice warm cognac and sharing a bag of chips. It was quite the combination. Tired from our day of being tourists, we went to bed early, looking forward to an early start in my real estate venture. I was simply focused on Estelle's house. I was not interested in any other property.

Estelle was pleased to see us again. I asked her if we could look at the house one more time, just as a formality, before telling her that I would buy it. I didn't even want to negotiate the price. I felt it would be a big insult to Estelle's generous pricing.

We started with going upstairs. It was fitting, seeing as that is where we left off the first time because of being freaked out. Estelle stayed downstairs, preparing us a light lunch and tea. She wanted us to have privacy so that we could speak freely and honestly. As I was walking up the stairs, I felt a warm breeze pass near my left ear. I could almost hear a whisper saying my name. Patty's expression not changing reassured me that it went unnoticed. When we got to the bathroom door, I asked Patty to wait in the bedroom while I went in the bathroom alone. I wanted to see if I would feel something. I excused myself and shut the door. As I heard the click of the latch catching, I also heard the whisper again, breathing my name in my ear. I knew for sure right there and then that I was meant to be here and to purchase the house.

During our lunch with Estelle, I told her that I would indeed buy the house from her and that I would help her with her move to the residence. I knew that she was alone and would have had to hire someone to help her. She was surprised to the point of tears. I got up from my chair and hugged her while she cried. I also offered to keep her cat if the home wouldn't allow her to take it. She was so thankful and relieved that Mr. Pete the cat would stay in his home. I reassured Estelle that he would be well taken care of and that she could visit us any time.

After Patty and I got back to our room, I told her that when I was going up the stairs, a warm breeze hit my left ear, and I heard it whisper my name. Then again, in the bathroom, I heard my name and felt the warmth of the whisper in my ear. Then I started to cry as I told her that when I was consoling Estelle as she cried in my arms, I was also strongly feeling that she was consoling me as well. It was a feeling I had never experienced before, yet Estelle said nothing to make me feel that way.

Patty was packing and getting ready for me to take her to the airport. The week had flown by so quickly. She was now flying out of Levis, which was the closest airport to us. Levis was less than an hour away. Her flight was leaving at five pm, which gave us lots of time to go onto Levis' streets and enjoy the time we had left by eating, walking around downtown, and having a drink before saying our goodbyes. I was staying in St Magloire for as long as it took to finalize the purchase and settle Estelle in her new home.

I met with the local attorney for the purchase of the house. I had to sign a conflict-of-interest release due to the fact that she was also Estelle's lawyer and the only lawyer in the village. It would take less than a week for the deal to be final and the property to be mine. I assured Estelle that she could take her time moving out of the house and that she could take anything she wanted from the house. I even offered to take her shopping for furniture for her new room along with anything else she would like to shop for. She was grateful for the offer but said that all she wanted from the house was an old handmade bassinet with a doll dressed in a beautiful baptismal gown made of satin. She did, however, take me up on the shopping excursion to Levis.

Estelle insisted I move into the house even though she was still living there. I was okay with that, also. We would get to know each other, and with my being there, I could help her pack her personal things and clothes. I would also be there with her to help her with this transition.

A week went by like a blink of an eye. We were finished packing into boxes things that Estelle and I wanted to give to the Salvation Army Thrift shop, and filling bags for garbage pick-up. This gave me room for when I came with some of my belongings from Nova Scotia.

Sunday afternoon, while we were having a cup of tea and scones, the priest from the church next door came to pay us a visit. I had never been introduced to him before though we did wave to each other a few times. Estelle had such a beaming smile on her face as soon as Father Paul entered the house, which just warmed my heart. He was the only person I saw give Estelle the time of day. My entire time ever since I had been at the house with Estelle, not once did her phone ring or someone came to the door.

Father Paul welcomed me to the village and invited me to visit him any time if I needed help or wanted company. He stayed with us for over two hours, enjoying himself, it seemed especially eating the muffins fresh out of the oven. Father Paul shook my hand at the door as he was leaving and held my gaze a little longer than normal. I did feel a little uncomfortable. It was as though he was trying to see inside me. Then he smiled and left.

I didn't feel comfortable asking Estelle about her solitude or anything about the villagers. I would find out things at my own pace and patience. I wasn't the friendly type myself and might put them off as well, which was fine by me. Maybe that was the same thing for Estelle. She had left the village for many years.

I went up early for a nice bath in my large claw foot tub and then called Patty. I wanted to share the events of my day along with the feelings that the day created. I was having restless nights again, and when I would awake after one of my dreams, I swear I heard someone crying. I would get up to listen at the top of the stairs to see if Estelle was all right, but all I would find was peaceful silence. It would take me forever to fall back asleep.

My one dream had Estelle's bassinet in it, with a live baby lying naked in its center, crying while the bassinet rocked on its own. I figured that dream to be because we had talked about Estelle taking the bassinet with her when she moved into the home.

Patty didn't call me back even though I had left a message on her phone when she didn't answer. I was looking forward to having a nice long conversation with her to help clear my head for a good night's sleep. If I don't hear from her in the next few days, I will call back for a longer chat for sure by then.

Today, Estelle and I are going to Levis shopping. Estelle's room at the home was freshly painted and ready for her to make it her home. We were looking for curtains with some lilac and green in them and hopefully some matching bedding. Estelle also picked out a nice oak single bed and matching dresser, and bed table. She also found a nice rocking chair that she would put next to her window. This would all be delivered in three days. Estelle was ecstatic. She said that she could not remember the last time she had so much fun. She simply beamed.

I took Estelle across by ferry to Old Quebec City. The day was still young, and I loved Old Quebec. We spent the rest of the afternoon being tourists and going into all the shops and museums. I took Estelle to the Chateau Frontenac for supper. That's when Estelle told me that she worked there for 40 years. She started as a receptionist at the front desk and became manager of all front-line staff. She was in charge of sixty-five employees for over 25 of those years. I was glad that I took her there to be wined and dined in a style she had witnessed many times.

We got back to the village after nine pm. It was a great day out but a long one. Estelle went straight to bed, and I poured myself a nice glass of brandy and sat on the front porch relaxing and enjoying the evening. I felt so much at home. A rare feeling for me.

For the next few days, Estelle and I put her room together in no time. The floor nurse, Claire, came over and gave Estelle papers to read and sign. She was all business and not friendly at all, which I found odd. After Estelle had read and signed the papers, I took them to the nurse's office to give them to Claire. She greeted me with a warm smile and took the papers from my hand. I told her that I could be called if Estelle needed anything and gave her my number. I noticed that her demeanor changed a bit at the mention of Estelle's name. I was getting puzzled at the reactions I was encountering and, honestly, a little upset. Claire saw the change in my face to her reaction and put a nice smile on as she took my information. The puzzlement didn't leave my face as I turned and walked away.

With Estelle, all settled in her new home and me alone in mine, I allowed myself a day of loud music while I made the house my own. I cleaned and rearranged, and baked, all the while singing and sipping a nice glass of Merlot. I'm sure the neighbors were not impressed. The music was loud, and the windows were open.

As I was shaking a rug outside on the front porch, the neighbor came out of her house and expressed how much she liked my choice of music and came over to introduce herself properly. She said that her name was Justine, and her husband's name was Louie Dostie. She welcomed me to the neighborhood and invited me for tea whenever. I told her that Estelle had just moved out and that I was moving things around and cleaning. I was taken aback when Justine said that she was happy that Estelle was gone and that she would not be missed. I was so stunned that I just politely took my leave and went inside. I even shut the music off. The mood was gone.

I took myself for a walk in the cemetery. I had some thinking to do, and I feel most comfortable in cemeteries and churches. I was standing over my grandfather's grave when the priest came up behind me and startled me. He saw that I was troubled by something and brought me to the rectory for a coffee and a chat.

Shortly after entering the den, Sister Marie-Jacques brought us coffee and biscuits and then excused herself. After the door closed behind her, I blurted out to Father Paul, "Why is Estelle hated by her neighbors and the nurse in the home? Does no one like her?" I was so angry that I had tears in my eyes, ready to escape any moment. My reaction even puzzled me. Father Paul shook his head and looked down at his hands, then said that he felt that Estelle was unjustly judged a long, long time ago, and the villagers were very unforgiving. "They call her a liar." When I asked why he simply shook his head and refused to answer, I saw in his eyes that he was bothered by this too.

I felt awful. Poor Estelle. Yet she never showed that anything bothered her about the way she was greeted and treated. All I saw was a gentle, non-threatening woman who minded her own business and bothered no one. I'm a good judge of people, and my intuitions have never been wrong. I honestly believe that Estelle has hurt no one, at least not enough, to deserve such shunning and disrespect. I believe that she is the person she portrays to be. She is gentle, honest, and very generous with her tolerance.

I went inside the church after my talk with Father Paul. I have always found comfort and peace in empty churches. Having people in there with me ruins the experience and atmosphere.

I sat in silent prayer for a while. I had to work through these emotions. I knew myself too well, and I didn't want to say or do anything that might further alienate the villagers from Estelle or cause them to take it out on her even more. I had to do a lot of thinking.

When I got home from my meditation, I made a few calls to friends in Nova Scotia. I was going to collect on some favors. I wanted to stay in St Magloire as long as I could. My house in Nova Scotia would have to be winterized when the weather changed. For now, the fridge had to be cleaned out of perishables, and my mail had to be redirected to me here in Quebec. I knew that by asking Perry and Sandra to do these things for me that I had nothing to worry about. They were both great friends, and they each had a key to go into the house. I then called the post office of my plans and the insurance broker. I was all set to stay as long as I needed. I had to get a few things settled here as well. I ordered internet service along with cable. I got myself organized for the long run.

After dinner, I went to the home to visit Estelle. Claire was on the floor and waved hello at me from the other end of the hall. I went into Estelle's room and was surprised when I saw that she had been crying. Right away, I knelt down next to her rocking chair to comfort her and ask her what had brought on these tears. She immediately put a brave smile on her face and said that she was just thinking about the past and her family. She felt alone and missed them very much. I told her that I understood her feeling this way and that she could call on me anytime if she got too lonely. I told her that she was a welcome in my life and my only friend out here. I asked her if she wanted to go on a day trip with me tomorrow to Levis. The pain in her eyes was replaced with a beam of glee. I told her that I would pick her up near ten.

On my way out, I stopped and talked to Claire. I said that it upset me to see Estelle crying alone in her room. I asked Claire if anything had happened to bring this on. She said that she was not aware of anything. I also said to Claire that I wanted to be told when Estelle was not well or when she was crying. I was going to be her contact person, and that I would get Estelle to draw up legal papers to that effect. I also made it clear that I expected respect for Estelle and me. I couldn't do anything about how they felt, but I could make sure that Estelle was no longer disrespected. I made my expectations very clear. Claire said that she would pass the word around and that she agreed that respect was needed. I was pleased with her attitude and answers.

On our way to Levis the next morning, I asked Estelle if she wanted me to be her contact person for legal and medical situations. I told her that I would be honored to act in that capacity if she felt comfortable with that. She reached and took my hand and just said, "Thank you. I would love that." I told her that I would make arrangements for us to meet with our mutual attorney and draw up the necessary papers.

When we got to Levis, I got my shopping out of the way and then treated Estelle to a day of beauty. We went to the spa for a massage and manicure, pedicure, and facial. We then went to the hairdresser in the mall and got our hair done. After we were as beautiful as we could be, we found the fanciest restaurant and had supper. The expression on Estelle's face was pure delight. It made me happy that I could cheer her up with this special day.

Claire was true to her word. Whenever I was with Estelle, all the staff were polite and greeted Estelle with respect. I noticed that even some of the residents were smiling and greeting Estelle as we walked by. It wasn't all warm and fuzzy, but it was so much better than before. Estelle looked more relaxed too.

I soon got into a daily routine. After my morning coffee, I would walk over to the home and have a short visit with Estelle. Then I would work out in the yard, making flower gardens in the front and back. When the weather got in my way, I would either work inside on some project or go for a long drive in the neighboring villages. I would even cook and bake so that I could stock my freezer for the winter. Winters are pretty wild here in this part of Quebec. I made a batch of cream puffs and took them to have with Estelle at the home. She had said once that they were her favorite. I wanted to surprise her for her birthday and got there in the middle of the dinner hour. I brought enough to share with whoever wanted some. When I got there, I saw that Estelle was missing from the dining room. Claire was not working, but the other staff all knew me, and when I asked the LPN where Estelle was, she simply said that Estelle refused to come out of her room and insisted on having her dinner there. She didn't say more than that.

When I got to Estelle's room, I saw that she had her supper in there instead of with the other residents. I asked her why she was eating in her room alone, and on her birthday, day of all days. She said that it was her choice and that this was where she wanted to eat. She seemed defiant and distant to me. I knew better than to push her, so I just gave her a few cream puffs, wished her a happy birthday, and hugged her on my way out.

When I left the home I went to the rectory, armed with cream puffs and ready to insist on some answers, hopefully over tea. Father Paul seemed happy to see me but more pleased to see the treat in my hands. We sat and enjoyed our dessert before I got into why I was here unannounced. I told him about the talk I had had with Claire a few weeks ago and that things were comfortable for Estelle and better than they had been. I also told him that I was now Estelle's contact person, armed with a power of attorney and executor to her last wishes.

I thought that I had put a stop to the disrespect and shunning that Estelle was receiving at the home. I saw that when I arrived unexpectedly, I found Estelle eating in her room alone, and her attitude was very unfriendly. I said that I wanted to know why Estelle was treated so badly. Father Paul said that he was not at liberty to say anything more than he already had but that he would go see Estelle the next day to look into the situation and to ask Estelle what he could share with me if anything. I was satisfied with his answer and told him that I expected to talk with him tomorrow.

Another restless night with troubling dreams. I was getting used to waking up upset in the middle of the night. I knew that I would have to look into the reason behind these nightmares. I needed to talk to a professional. This time the dreams were deeper.

I awoke to crying sounds coming from the den downstairs. It sounded like a baby crying. As I was going down the stairs, I heard my name again whispered and I couldn't make out the rest of what it said as I felt its breeze pass by my ear. I entered the den and turned on the light, and saw that the bassinet was rocking and the crying had stopped. As I bent down to look at the doll in the bassinet, I noticed that it was face down, and it started crying again. Then I woke up and sat up like a tight spring in my own bed. I could hear my heart pounding, and I was trembling. I was scared for the first time in my house. Even Mr. Pete was edgy.

After my second cup of coffee, I went to the senior's home to ask Estelle a few questions. When I got to her room, I could hear a woman's voice being quite stern with Estelle. I didn't bother announcing my presence and opened the door to see the LPN, Marie-Anne, scolding Estelle. I told her to get out, and I followed her into the hall. I was furious and in no mood for excuses and bullshit. I demanded an explanation! Marie-Anne said that she was tired of Estelle's lies, and she finally called her on it. I asked her to tell me what she meant by that accusation.

"Estelle has been a pathological liar for years. Everyone knows that. Now her new lies include you in them. She said that you were born in that house and that she prayed you hear, and you miraculously appeared. How many lies do we have to put up with? It's not a part of our job description to be made fools of."

I felt such a rage come over me. I looked Marie-Anne square in the face and told her through clenched teeth that I was indeed born in that house on February 5th, 1954. My maiden name is Celine Thibault. My parents were Xavier and Valerie Thibault. Marie-Anne just blanched.

I guess I was speaking with force because Claire showed up on the run to see what the hell was going on. I told her that I had caught Marie-Anne bullying Estelle, and she was calling her a liar. I said, with as much authority I could voice, that I would not put up with Estelle being mistreated or disrespected again and that I intended to report this incident to the proper authorities. Marie-Anne was dumbfounded hearing that Estelle was indeed telling the truth. I was born in that house and did buy it exactly like

Estelle had said. Claire's face registered surprise as she mentioned Marie-Anne's name in disgust.

I left them standing in the hall with their red faces and mixed expressions and walked home. I was way too angry to stay a minute longer. I would deal with this after I calmed down. My anger would only make matters worse for Estelle.

A couple of hours after I got home, there was a knock at the front door. It was Father Paul. Estelle had called him and told him what had happened. He said that Estelle felt responsible. I told him that my anger was not directed at Estelle and that she held no blame for Marie-Anne's unacceptable behavior. I did, however, ask him how Estelle knew who I was. I had not shared that with anyone. That's when he came and sat next to me on the sofa and handed me a key.

He asked for a drink…something with a kick. I poured us a glass of cognac. He explained that the key opened a secret box under the peacock just above the bathtub. He said that what I would find there would cause me to have many questions. He didn't want to get into it until I had had a chance to see all the contents, and he made me promise to do nothing for at least twenty-four hours. He said that I would need time to absorb and compose myself before I spoke to him about it. He asked that I not bring this up with Estelle for the time being. She was not aware that he was going to do this while she was still alive. He assured me that he would answer any and all questions after the twenty-four-hour cooling period. He also said that I should be alone through this and talk to no one.

After Father Paul left, I walked over to the home to see if Estelle was all right. I was worried that my outburst might have caused her grief or put her in a worse position with the staff and residents of the home. When I got there, Estelle was sitting in the common room with another resident. They were chatting amicably over a cup of tea. I walked over and sat on the chair facing them. Estelle introduced the woman as Mme. Tanguay. I politely shook Mme. Tanguay's hand and said that I was pleased to meet her. Estelle then got up, and we excused ourselves and went to Estelle's room. Once the door was closed, Estelle turned to me and gave me such a big hug. She thanked me for coming to her defense and for not being angry at her for omitting the fact that she knew who I was all along. I cried with relief.

We had a nice talk. I got to hear a bit about her childhood and my parents. She also shared a few of her memories of me. I was captivated by her stories. The timing was right for me to ask her a few questions that played on my mind.

"Estelle, I have had a few dreams with the bassinet in them; what significance would the bassinet have to me?"

"As you know, I grew up next door to your house, and I knew your parents and grandfather. Your father had made the bassinet himself. The doll in it was your gift from my mother when you were born. The outfit on the doll is the one you were baptized in. I knew that one day you would come back and that I could give those to you."

I felt feelings inside me that I had never thought possible to feel. I couldn't think straight. I felt the need to run out of there. Not that I was upset with Estelle, but I just didn't know how to act or react. I thanked her for her candid answer and told her that I had to leave but that I was okay.

I also told her that I would not be able to visit her for a few days and that I would see her as soon as I could.

What a day! My head was spinning. My outburst at the home towards Marie-Anne had opened up a Pandora's Box. All this was happening like in a dream. Was I dreaming? I knew I was awake because my chess was so tight that I thought it would crack open and spill my nervous guts all over the living room floor. The bassinet...the fight...the questions...the ANSWERS! I was afraid to move, fearing what might happen next. There was no way that I could attempt the secret box today. I called the rectory and spoke with Sister Marie-Jacques and asked her to tell Father Paul that I would be taking 48 hours instead of 24 and that he would understand what it meant. I then poured myself a stiff brandy and sat on the porch with my thoughts and a warm jacket. It was mid-September already, and for here that meant cooler evenings.

Oh no! Again, not with the dreams... I woke up just as dawn was breaking. I was startled awake by a voice in my dream. At least, I think it was in my dream. I lay there motionless for a while to listen and see if any noise was coming from my awake state. All was quiet except for Mr. Pete purring loudly on my shoulder. I started petting him, and he rolled onto his back to get more affection. We stayed there relaxed in the quiet of the room and of the house, and we both went back to sleep until late morning.

It was raining outside with the occasional flash of lightning followed by a distant clap of thunder. I loved stormy days. They calmed me down and gave me such peace. All was well in my life during a storm. I took myself downstairs for a nice cup of coffee and sat in front of the dining room window, where I had set up bird feeders just outside. There were a few cardinals with their feathers sticking out in all directions from being wet by the rain. There was also a lone sparrow keeping himself out of the rain standing directly under the feeder's floor. I thought to myself, "What better day to explore these new happenings in my life." I brought my coffee and the key with me and went to the upstairs bathroom.

I sat at the edge of the tub in silent prayer, asking God to prepare me for whatever this was that was waiting for me. I felt at peace and emotionally strong, so I proceeded to open the secret compartment under the peacock. It was almost full to the top with pictures, papers, and envelopes. I reached inside and took a handful of its content out, and brought it to my bed. I lay it all in front of me. Mr. Pete thought he could help by laying over top of everything, making it impossible to see properly what it was that I was looking at. I decided to put him out and shut the bedroom door.

There were pictures of a baby and some of a toddler, along with a much younger Estelle. There were pictures of my father and a few adults I didn't know. There were pictures of that same baby in the bassinet, which I can just assume were of me. I surprised myself when I started crying uncontrollably. Finally…baby pictures of me…pictures of me growing into a toddler, pictures of me in my father's arms while he beamed down at me. Pictures that held the love I missed, the history I didn't have. Picture of my friend Estelle in her youth.

I must have looked at those same contents for over an hour, crying off and on. What a gift this was to me. I felt ready for more. What was left in the box? I took another handful and brought that to the bed for me to spread it out. There were a few newspaper clippings of me along with my career achievements. There were pictures of my wedding, which took place in Niagara Falls in 1976. There was my mother and brother. My husband Samuel Drake with hair! We looked so different, so...unhappy! That was puzzling. I thought it had been a good day. Funny how nerves hide reality.

I had had enough of my wedding pictures. How did Estelle know about who I was in my career? How did she get these...how did she know? Just a handful of trusted people knew my secret identity. No one else had a clue; I made sure of that. How did Estelle Garand, from this small village in Quebec, get pictures of me displaying all my accomplishments from all over the world? There were ticket stubs and concert brochures, and programs written in at least four different languages from different countries. How!?

I went back to the box, hoping for answers in another handful. There were a few bundles of opened letters tied together with ribbons which were from my cousin, Jasmine, who lived in Ontario. Jasmine? She knows, Estelle? I took a bundle and carefully undid the ribbon and opened one letter at a time, and read its contents. As I sat there in disbelief and shock, I heard the whisper of my name again and felt a breeze coming from what seemed to be the window with the peacock. I stood there and looked at it, not really seeing it as I was in a daze. Looking down, I saw at the bottom of the box the picture I had used for my tattoo. I had found that picture in a National Geographic, and there was a copy of it. This was the only tattoo that I got after being in Nova Scotia for a year. How long had this woman been following my life, and why?

It was hard for me not to call Father Paul or talk to Estelle or even call Patty or Jasmine, for that matter. Twenty-four hours…no, forty-eight hours seemed like an impossible eternity. I just left everything on my bed and went for a walk in the rain. I went to the cemetery, and I stood there among my relatives and strangers…No peace! No answers! I went and sat in the church, praying for enlightenment. Again, I found no peace, no answers. Even sitting for a long time in the still of the church where so many prayers had reached the ears of God…No peace…No answers.

I walked by the senior's home and stood outside in the pouring rain, just looking at the building. The building housed the woman with all the answers to these overwhelming mysteries, which involved what seemed to be my entire life. I felt so alone and lost with nowhere to go. I went back to my house and sat on the porch in the rain, letting the weather wash over me. I was alone in this for at least 48 hours. I looked at the time, and five hours had passed already, so we were down to 43 hours. That was no relief to me. Might as well have been 43 days. It all felt like an eternity.

Someone calling out to me broke into my thoughts. It was Justine, the neighbor, who had expressed her hatred of Estelle. She half laughingly asked me why I was sitting in the rain…was I locked out of the house? I gave her a leering look and silently went inside. I had no time or patience for her kind. I poured myself a nice hot bath to get the chill out of my bones from being soaked right through. As I lay warming up in the tub, I kept staring at the peacock in the stained-glass window, hoping to understand what was going on, what it all meant. Praying for answers to break into the silence of my thoughts, I felt peace within my stormy adventure. I was more unnerved but, at the same time, intrigued.

I decided to be productive as though it was any other normal day. I cleaned the bathrooms and decided to make a large pot of soup. I was hoping that by keeping busy, it would calm my spirit and open my understanding or give me some discernment. When I saw that my absent-mindedness was causing danger to my digits, I put the knife down and the vegetables away and thought better than to make soup. My concentration was elsewhere, and I had stalled long enough. I couldn't escape or avoid these new findings, and I had less than forty hours to get all of my questions on paper so that Father Paul could answer every single one of them. I went to the box and emptied the remaining contents. There were just a few items left. The entire findings were on my bed. I took the letters out of the opened envelopes to read first. They were all from my cousin Jasmine whom I wasn't that close to, really. The last time I spoke to Jasmine was when I had closed my affairs in Ontario and was ready to leave for my new life in Nova Scotia. I had lunch with her and our other cousin Irene.

Most of the letters in the first bundle I opened were from a much younger Jasmine. They dated back to the 1940s. I didn't spend too much of my fleeting time on those. The first letter I read from the second bundle was dated the year my father died. A year that drastically changed my life.

September 19, 1959
My dear friend Estelle;

I have some bad news to share with you. I know that this information would interest you. Xavier Thibault died this week from a work-related accident. My parents are with the family now, so they are not alone. There are a few of us cousins from both sides of the family here staying nearby to help the family through this tragedy.

I will write to you again soon. Hope that you are well, and if you need me, I am here.

Your friend
Jasmine

Included in the envelope was my father's death notice from the newspaper along with the letter. This I could understand; after all, Estelle knew my family back then. The next letter was from later that same year.

December 20, 1959
Merry Christmas, Estelle.

I was so happy to hear from you. It must be very busy in Old Quebec this time of year with the winter carnival. I remember you telling me how much you enjoy the Santa Clause parade.

We are planning to meet at my aunt Lena's house after midnight mass on Christmas Eve. We take turns hosting the traditional celebratory meal, and this year it's Lena's turn. Lena is Valerie's first cousin. Don't know if you would remember her. They lived on the rural number six route outside the village.

Valerie, Richard, and Celine seem to be coping well enough with this being their first Christmas without Xavier and the end of this difficult year just around the corner. Richard never leaves his mother's side. Celine keeps to herself and is very quiet. It's a little spooky to see a five-year-old so quiet. They are never alone for long. We all take turns inviting them to our home or bringing them food. I make it a point to go at least once a week, and I take the kids out for a ride and a treat. Celine doesn't say much. She's taking it the hardest, I think. She's always alone when I see her.

Hope you're well and have a very Merry Christmas.

*Your friend
Jasmine.*

I have no memories of that Christmas or of any for that matter. Even when I looked at the pictures, I had just found out about us so nothing came to mind. They are just pictures with me in them of a forgotten time of my life. Even though the photos put me and my family there in the darkness of my remembrance. Every now and again, I get a fleeting memory that just leaves behind a feeling before I can even grasp and hold on to it.

July 2, 1961
Hello Estelle;

We will be in St Magloire on the 22nd of this month. We are bringing Valerie and her children for a visit. We will be doing the rounds to all the relatives on both sides of the family. We will be staying three days in St Magloire and three days in Armagh before going on to Quebec City for a week. It would be nice to see you.

Nothing much is happening here. My job is still boring, and Jack still drinks too much, and the dog has kidney stones. Other than that, life is uneventful. Take care, my friend, and see you soon.

Jasmine.

I will inquire how Estelle and Jasmine got to know each other enough to be friends. It's not that much of a stretch, really, because Estelle and her family lived next door to us in the village, but it is nagging at me the connection between the two. Jasmine's family had moved to Ontario before us, and they are not related, so how did they get to be friends?

August 27, 1961
My dear Estelle

I can't say it enough, how nice it was to see you again. You've not changed that much in 13 years. I did miss your beautiful long hair, but, short also looks good on you.

Estelle, I know what the Thibault family means to you and that you seem to have a special place in your heart for Celine. As do I. She has been pushed aside and left alone far too much since her father passed away. I give her special attention every time I go and visit, but I know it's not enough. That being said, I am puzzled by something, and I apologize ahead of time for my boldness, but I must ask. Is Celine your sister?

When I walked into the living room and Celine was sitting on your lap, you both looked up at me at the same time, and I couldn't help but notice that Celine was a younger version of you. The resemblance is far too striking for the two of them not to be related.

I hope that I have not overstepped the parameters of our friendship or have offended you in any way. My intentions are not malicious. Do keep well, and I look forward to your letter...with or without an answer to my forwardness.

Jasmine

Though I personally didn't see any resemblance between Estelle and me, Jasmine's questioning her so personally in that letter created such a tightness in my chest that I thought I was going to be sick. I got up from the bed and started pacing the room like a condemned person waiting on death row for the inevitable. My heart was pounding so hard that I felt every pulse in my body. With shaky hands, I have no choice but to push on and get through this. Whatever this is.

September 20, 1961
Thank you for your letter, Estelle.

I was relieved to hear from you in such a short time. Thank you for not being upset with me. Your friendship has meant so much to me all these years.

I never thought for a million years that Celine was your daughter. How sad I feel for you and for all you've lost. I see how much you love her. It must have been so difficult to lose her when the family moved away. I am beyond finding the right words to express myself to you in this matter.

You've nothing to blame yourself for. You were only sixteen when you got pregnant. A mere child yourself. Xavier did right by you from what you wrote. This explains so much. I promise to keep your privacy intact, and your painful sacrifice is safe with me. I want to help you as much as you will allow me. I will keep an eye on Celine and keep you informed of every step of her life as best I can.

Thank you for your trust and true friendship.
Jasmine

This can't be true. Estelle…my mother? My world just stopped, and all I see is black confusion. I feel like I'm going to pass out or be sick again. Estelle…and my father. NO! Oh, my dear God, I need your help right now. Please, Lord, help me!

When I came to, Mr. Pete was lying on me as I lay half on the bed where I had passed out. I still felt faint and weak. This did not just happen. I have never passed out in my entire life. Close at times, but NEVER!

I didn't care that I still had thirty hours to go before asking any questions or seeing anyone. I ran to the rectory as I was still in my PJs and pounded on the door. I was near panic when Sister Marie-Jacques answered the door. I told her that I needed to speak with Father Paul right away. She said that Father Paul gave her instructions to tell me that it was not time yet and to go home and stay there until tomorrow evening. He would call on me when the time was right and not before.

I could not believe how cruel Father Paul was! There he was, looking at me through the window, motionless. I screamed as loudly as I could muster up the words. "I can't do this alone. Please, please help me!" Then I saw him turn away from the window as Sister Marie-Jacques quietly closed the door.

I had no choice but to go back to my house. What else could I do? I have never felt so alone and helpless. I am not a stranger to pain, but this surpassed anything I had ever felt. I went in and poured myself a stiff brandy and then another, and then out I was. This time the alcohol took me away.

When I woke up, it was nearly noon the next day. I felt like I should have died. This was a hangover to teach other hangovers how it's done. It wasn't my heart or my spirit which were hurting anymore. It was my entire being. No way was this the body I was familiar with. I was literally scared to move in fear of my head falling off and landing in the vomit that would precede its fall by a mere second. Never again!

Out of an overwhelming helplessness in this situation, I started to cry like a wounded child. I do remember sitting on Estelle's lap when I was six. I thought that she was the nicest person for giving me some attention. I also remember that she had given me a little blue and gold music box with a crank on the side. I loved that gift more than I had ever loved anything before. I felt so special. I have never forgotten that feeling. I listened to that music box for hours by myself. My mother…Valerie took it away from me because it was getting on everyone's nerves, hearing it over and over. I never saw it again.

After a strong coffee and dry toast, I went back upstairs to go through everything that had been in the box. I read the opened letters which contained events of my life, I looked at the pictures of me from baby to toddler, and I fell in love with this child who was indeed loved way back when. There I was in the bassinet, made by my father's hands; some pictures were of me laying on my back but mostly on my stomach. There were photographs of my baptism. I was held in Valerie's arms, with my father by her side and Estelle standing next to the priest. My favorite one was of me sitting on my dad's lap. I was looking at him with a smile on my face, and he was looking down at me with pride in his eyes. I felt it in my heart as though it was happening at this very moment.

There were no pictures of me with Valerie other than my baptism. In fact, there was only one picture of her alone in the entire collection. It was of her standing behind an ornate counter with snow globes on a shelf behind her. I didn't recognize the place it had been taken. She looked the same as before she died, just younger. The sternness in her look, which had never changed for as long as I could remember, was engraved on this photograph. I bet I could count the times I saw her smile.

It warmed my heart to see these images of me. There had been none of me as a baby or toddler until now. The earliest pictures of me that I had seen were taken when I was four years old. The first one was of me standing next to my father with my finger near my mouth and a shy look on my face. There were a lot of people sitting around the table, drinking beer and playing cards. My dad had his arm around me. The next ones were of the three of us standing in front of a grave marker with my father's name on it. That was a family picture with our faces like the stone which marked where my father rested. And the saddest picture was of me standing at the end of the driveway where we lived back in 1959, alone, with such sadness in my eyes. Come to find out that it was taken the day of my dad's funeral. My heart always broke for that sad little girl...me!

I have so many questions, and I am putting so much hope into the answers. Though I do have some answers to questions I have asked myself all my life just by exploring the contents of this box. This explains some of what I lived and why it was that way for me. I always had a roof over my head and food to eat, but it stopped there. I was feeling such a loss, a deep emptiness right now. If Estelle is really my mother, it explains why Valerie was so distant and cold towards me all my life.

I finally read the last letter which was sent to Estelle by Jasmine. It had Valerie's obituary notice in it. Jasmine told Estelle that Valerie was gone and that maybe now would be a good time to reach out to me and claim her place in my life. She even offered to be involved in the process if Estelle needed her. I said to myself aloud, "That won't be necessary, Jasmine...I now know."

There was a large manila envelope folded in half with newspaper clippings, concert ticket stubs, and programs from all over Canada and the world. It had my brother Richard's return address on the front of it. Apparently, he had kept Estelle in the know as well. He never gave any indication that he knew my truth and that he was in contact with Estelle. There was a short note that simply said, "I thought you might like to have these of my sister's accomplishments." It was signed by Richard Thibault.

Estelle knew that CiCi Pascale was my stage name. Not too many people were privy to this information. I always performed in costume, wearing a mask. I never allowed myself to be interviewed in person. It would only be over the phone or through my agent, nor did I sign autographs after my shows. I would always leave after the last song while still in costume. My limo would be at the ready before the last note left my voice.

The memories were flowing like an engorged river. Would I have been CiCi Pascale if I was Valerie's biological daughter? Would I have had the career I had for over thirty years if I would have stayed with Estelle? The life I had lived made me who I was and who I became. My career was my escape and my protection. If people knew that I was CiCi Pascale, would I have still been loved and accepted?

I had one more envelope to open. This one was still sealed, and it had my name on it. I chose not to open it alone. I would wait for Father Paul to be with me to see its contents and only after I got answers to my many questions. I wasn't even tempted to read it. Later this evening would be soon enough.

The time has arrived. Father Paul should be coming to my door any minute now. I made us a nice cake pudding and a strong pot of coffee. I think that it's going to be a long evening.

The knock on the door came right on time, as expected. Father Paul came armed with a nice bottle of Remi-Martin Cognac. That was a sign that we were in for a bumpy ride, but I was ready and very nervous.

My words made me sound a lot more in control than I felt inside. I didn't waste any time. I poured us a cognac and a coffee and sat us both in the living room for maximum comfort. The dessert treat would have to wait. I asked the first question that came to mind. I figured the others would easily follow. The way I felt, I knew that I wouldn't omit one question until I had all the answers, along with all the details needed to calm my spirit. I was a mess inside.

"How was it that my father got Estelle pregnant? She was only sixteen. That's statutory rape."

"Estelle lived next door to your parents. She helped your mother with her ailing father and sometimes took care of your brother Richard. Valerie had to take Richard for tests in Rimouski, which was a few hours away, and would have to stay overnight for results and follow-ups. He had been feeling poorly, and the local doctor suspected allergies. Your father worked in the woods close by with other villagers, and so Estelle stayed with Joseph, Valerie's father, while Xavier was at work. She prepared supper for your dad and stayed until she could clear the table and washed the supper dishes. This was not the first time that Estelle was asked to help.

Your father arrived later than usual this particular evening. He had been drinking, which was a rare event for him. Come to find out the next day that he was upset thinking that he had killed a man. This man was a real pain in the neck to everybody who met him. He was a loudmouth, ignorant sot. It took a lot to get your dad angry, but this man, Roland Menard, I believe he was called, pushed your father to his limit. They were driving home together from the next village, in the company mini-bus, along with two other men from St Magloire. Roland started saying that he could get any married woman he wanted. That he could give them what they needed from a real man. Your father told him to be quiet and that he was being a jerk. Roland didn't know how to shut up. He then said that he could even have Valerie in bed simply by unbuckling his pants. Your father rose off his seat and backhanded Roland upside the head. Roland was knocked out cold and wouldn't come to. Your dad thought for sure he was dead. When the bus got to Roland's house, your father picked him up and brought him in the house, and laid him on the floor in front of the wood stove. Roland never moved or opened his eyes. Your father just left him there and went back to the bus.

The men on the bus were all uneasy and a little scared. The driver took them all to the tavern for a drink or two to calm them down. When Xavier got home, he continued to drink. He refused to eat supper, so Estelle was putting the food away and was cleaning up when your father went to her and made advances. Estelle was naïve, and she had had a crush on your father for a long time. She often said that she wanted a husband just like him when she got married.

It happened only once, and your father told Valerie what had happened when she got home, and they both spoke to Estelle together. They apologized for his behavior and promised that it would never happen again.

Estelle found out a couple of months later that she was pregnant. It was agreed by all that Estelle would give birth in their house and that they would tell everyone that Valerie had had the baby. Then Estelle would go away for a few weeks to make it look like she went away to have the baby that she was carrying and that she gave it up for adoption. It was the Catholic thing to do. This way, there was no need to involve anyone else, nor did they have to formally adopt the baby. The doctor and the priest at the time agreed that it was the best way to handle this unfortunate situation. It hid the scandal from the villagers. So, you see, you were never formally adopted by Valerie.

Estelle helped take care of you until you all moved away to Ontario. She loved you so very much. She was so broken up when you left her life. You see, Celine, you did have your mother's love from the day you were born. She told me that she would watch you sleep in your bassinet for hours. When she would leave to go home, she would lay you down on your stomach because you had a lot of mucus, and she didn't want you to choke."

"That explains a lot. It tells me why Valerie was always so distant. I became an invisible child after my father died. I remained invisible all of her life. Why am I finding this out now?"

"Your cousin Jasmine kept Estelle informed of you and your life. They had been friends ever since Janine and her family had visited when they were both seven. They remained pen-pals all those years. After Valerie passed away, your brother Richard sent Estelle a large envelope with revealing information about you.

After Valerie died four years ago, Estelle started praying for you to know the truth and maybe come home to her. She just wanted to see you. She figures that the truth will be revealed only after she herself dies. She didn't want this to happen just yet. She is so afraid to hurt you and lose you all over again."

"Who else knows about this? How did you find out? Did anyone in Ontario know besides Jasmine and Richard?"

"Your brother found out when he was 15. He overheard your mother talking to Jasmine's mother, Rita and confronted Valerie after Rita had left. He always knew there was a big secret that he had overheard many years before, but he was too young to remember or process what it all meant.

Then there's me; who knows? Estelle was so very much alone, and the villagers were mean to her and shunned her. She had no one to talk to, and she opened up to me one day when we were alone in the church. I took her under my wing and tried to be as good a friend as I could be. There are a few of the villagers that remain civil to Estelle but not when others are around.

Even Estelle's parents believe that she went away to have the baby and gave it up. Estelle stayed with Valerie's sister, Ava, in Valore for a month. When she came back alone, everyone believed that she had given her baby up for adoption, and no one ever knew who the father had been."

"Why are they so cruel towards Estelle now? I witnessed it a few times. It really pissed me off. I can't imagine her ever being a threat or hurtful to anyone."

"When Estelle moved back to the village after she retired from her years at Frontenac, she rented the apartment over the corner store and became good friends with Diane Menard, Roland's sister. Now Diane was about the only one who knew that Xavier had slugged her brother, which almost killed him. Roland never told anyone else who had bruised the entire left side of his face. Diane was a hateful woman. The whole family was minus a few cards in the deck. Nonetheless, Diane had great influence in the village because she was rich and ran the only store in St Magloire.

Estelle and Diane became best friends. Estelle would help out in the store, and they would go shopping in Quebec City and Levis and stay over in Rimouski. They were always going somewhere. Diane was the kind of woman who liked to be adored and obeyed, and she was the smartest, in her own opinion, and she had the best of everything. She was that type. Estelle, on the other hand, was not. She appreciated all that Diane did for her, thinking that Diane was a good friend. Diane, behind Estelle's back, was spreading rumors about Estelle and telling everyone all of Estelle's confidences. Estelle didn't stand a chance against Diane's malicious mouth.

One day Estelle told Diane that she knew what became of the child which she had out of wedlock. Though the entire village already knew that Estelle had had a child, they didn't know it all. She said that her daughter had become a famous singer known the whole world over. Estelle was so proud of you. CiCi Pascale…her star. She felt happy giving the world such a gift as you. So, she had trusted Diane with her most precious secret, believing that she was a friend. Diane took great pleasure in this bit of news and blew it up to a great big scandal. That's when Estelle was shunned and falsely accused of being a liar. Diane turned the villagers against her, telling them lies and fabrications. The villagers that didn't believe Diane or even like her also followed in shunning Estelle out of fear of what Diane might do to them.

Estelle moved out of Diane's apartment when she bought your house. They haven't spoken to each other ever since. It's been lonely and hard for Estelle."

This was a good time to take a bit of a break. I warmed up the cake pudding and made us a fresh pot of coffee. As we sat at the dining room table, I noticed that Father Paul had a distant look on his face. I asked him what was troubling him. He just said that he often cried a tear or two for Estelle. She is such a gentle soul who lost out on so much. He felt like he had failed Estelle by not standing up for her with the villagers. Even when he wanted to, Estelle would ask him not to.

I hadn't seen Estelle in a few days. She had called Father Paul to find out if something was wrong or if I was upset with her. He told her that I was feeling under the weather and not to worry. He said that I didn't want to spread whatever it was that I was fighting.

The time had come to bring out the unopened envelope. I told Father Paul that I didn't want to be alone when I looked at its contents. For some reason, I felt intimidated by this one. We went back to the living room with a nice glass of cognac and resumed the unfolding of truth.

"I have this envelope with my name on it, and I wanted you here when I opened it. I have gone through all the pictures and letters from Jasmine and her collections in my career, along with what Richard sent. I am thrilled to finally have baby and toddler pictures of me. I have never felt so many different feelings at once and yet so exhilarated. I have cried with depths unknown to me before. I even laughed in a glee at the love these pictures portrayed. I have no doubt that I was loved. But I cannot fully believe that

Estelle is my mother, yet I do. Can you understand that, Father?"

"The unopened envelope can help you with that. I know its contents, and I know that all your doubts will fade away."

"Before I open this envelope, please explain to me my dreams. Are they from God? I can think of no other explanation for them. I believe that they were instrumental in all these discoveries. I cannot count how frequently I had them. Each one would speak differently to me. Even while awake, I had strange things happen, like whispers and breezes. I honestly can't figure it all out, but I know that it brought me to this."

"Estelle and I prayed for many years for you. Whenever Estelle would hear from Jasmine, she would come over and share the news, and we would pray accordingly. After Valerie passed away, we prayed every morning. We asked God to intervene and to somehow bring you here. Estelle wanted to see you before she died. She is torn with her decision not to tell you the truth, but she is a selfless soul and doesn't want to upset you. She is so happy you are in her life, if only as a friend. She couldn't ask for more. You have made her so happy. She also doesn't want the villagers to hurt you and treat you badly as they've treated her. When you spoke out on her behalf a couple of weeks ago, she got very frightened that they would turn on you."

"I wouldn't advise it! I am not as gentle and forgiving as Estelle. I know now more than before that I will not tolerate their shunning or disrespect towards Estelle. This stops now!"

My anger was evident to the priest at my table. No way will I allow anyone to hurt Estelle ever again. I love her, and at this point, I don't care if she is or is not my mother. I will protect her. The look on Father Paul's face assured me that he was glad for Estelle and also for me.

"Please, Celine, would you now open the envelope?"

It was time for the final reveal. I opened the envelope and found a handwritten letter along with two formal sheets of paper with letterhead, giving the results of my brother's DNA test and blood type information and the other of Estelle's results. Their names, date of birth, blood type, and her unique DNAs. I then read the letter. There was also a blank request sheet for further testing with my name at the top.

"My dearest Celine;

As you read this in a state of bewilderment and confusion, please know that I never wanted to cause you pain. I do believe, though, that you have the right to know the truth. Your truth.

I was young when I got pregnant with you and I gave birth to a beautiful baby girl. I even got to name you Celine—a name I have always loved. I am so sorry to tell you like this, but I didn't want to disrupt your life, but then, Father Paul convinced me that it was your right to know.

Your father is really Xavier Thibault. Valerie, the mother who raised you, knew about what had happened between me and your father. We all worked it out, and forgiveness was accepted by all. Valerie agreed to claim you as her own. Her graciousness saved us all a lot of shame and pain. I'm sure she did it out of love for your father.

I went for a genetic test to give you proof of who I am. Your brother Richard also went for a DNA test for comparison to prove who your father was. Here is a form all filled out and paid for if you want to get yourself tested. You can go to the clinic in Rimouski with these papers, and you will know for sure, leaving you with no doubt.

All I ask now is that you forgive me for not being in your life. Forgive your father for his one moment of weakness, and forgive Valerie for not being able to love you the way you deserve to be. Know that you were the love of my life, and I thank God that I had you with me for the first two years of your life. It has made me happy for all of my years.

All my love.
Your mother, Estelle."

I was crying so hard that I was choking and heaving as though I was going to be sick. Father Paul was bent over me, holding me so tight that I couldn't move. I must have cried for an hour. It took me quite a while to get control of myself enough to even utter a word. I think I was crying for Estelle's pain. Her selfless sacrifices and the cruelty she had endured. Her loneliness…and, most of all, her gentle graciousness. I don't need a DNA test. I believe that she is my mother and that her love gave me a great beginning. I consider this information my greatest gift.

We sat in silence for a while after I had stopped walking. Father Paul had poured us another cognac. I looked at him and asked if I should tell Estelle that I knew the truth. He advised against it for now. He said that when the timing was right, I would know, and it would all fall into place and come to light.

We talked until half past one in the morning. I had another restless night of fitful sleeping. I woke up. It was still dark out, but dawn was about to break. I had a dream. In it, I heard the whisper again as I walked up the stairs, but this time it wasn't just my name I heard pass my ear; I clearly heard, "Celine, I love you forever and then some." Estelle's words to me. I know that now.

I got out of bed a few minutes before noon. I had fallen back to sleep just after dawn after my morning coffee. I got dressed and walked to the rectory to talk with Father Paul. I wanted to keep the connection we had created last evening. Sister Marie-Jacques brought us tea and left the room right away.

"I need to go away for a while. I will try to make it back for Christmas. I want to think away from here and absorb it all. I will come back. I will inform Estelle that I need to tie up some loose ends in Nova Scotia and that I will return for Christmas. Do you celebrate Midnight Mass here?"

"Yes. This year is our turn for the mass. The surrounding villages take turns each year, seeing as the population has declined so much, and that there are only two priests for the entire county. So, we take turns."

"I will ask Estelle to stay at the house and care for Mr. Pete. That will reassure her of my coming back, and that all is fine, in case she is wondering. I have been acting odd lately."

***

When it snowed in Quebec…it snowed. We awoke to the second blizzard in a week. There were snow banks of over ten feet in front of my house already. November was still a young month. If this keeps up, we will still have snow banks into July.

I made sure to go visit Estelle every day. I wanted to see her as often as I could. She didn't seem to suspect that I knew the truth, and I did my best not to act any differently around her. She knew that I was leaving in a few days and that I was indeed coming back. I was going to take her to the house the day before I left. She was worried about the weather interfering with the care of the property. I told her that Father Paul was going to keep an eye on her and that I had hired someone to clear the porches and the driveway. I assured her that I was just a phone call away.

I still needed to process and accept these revelations in the freedom of space that would not upset Estelle. That was one of the reasons I planned to leave in November. It also made it easier on me knowing she was to stay at the house for that long and care for Mr. Pete the entire time I was gone. I was reassured also knowing that Father Paul was just next door and he had volunteered to keep a vigilant eye on things.

I arrived in Nova Scotia on a Friday and stayed just long enough to tie up loose ends. I had to go to Ontario and see Patty and talk to her face to face. I had told her some of what was going on, but the meat of it was not yet said to her. I also needed her help.

I got to Patty's home the following Tuesday. We had a nice supper at home and sat in front of the fireplace to drink our dessert. It was a nice rich Merlot from Cote du Rhone.

I brought the pictures and letters out to show her. She's the only one who could help me through this. She is my most stable friend, and I trust her opinions.

Patty was very quiet while going through the pictures. She would look up at me from time to time as though I wasn't there. She was deep in thought. At one point, she said, to herself mostly, that the eyes are the same. As she was looking at the contents, I would talk every now and then to break the uncomfortable silence. Finally, Patty put everything down and said that now we could talk about all of this and about what I thought it means to me.

"Do you believe that Estelle is your biological mother? And are you going for the DNA testing?"

"Yes! I do believe that Estelle is my mother, and no, on the DNA test, as it would not change my mind. This woman loved me as a baby, and I have proof of my importance and existence because of her love for me. That's enough for me.

How fantastic is this, hey? My entire existence has a different meaning. I still feel a bit outside my life right now but the balance will come back, and I am ready to embrace the changes.

I want to do something special for Estelle. Try and make up a bit for all she's lost. I want to use my celebrity to elevate her in the eyes of the village. I want to shame those who have been cruel and dismissive of her for so many years. I truly want them to feel it!"

"That would mean going public with your identity. The great mystery of "Who is CiCi Pascale" would be solved, and you would live visibly in your fame."

"I've been retired long enough that it would only be a brief headline, and it would fade quickly. I'm willing to take the chance. I am going to solicit Father Paul's help and of course, I need your help too. I can't do it alone."

"I'm in! So, what's your big reveal looking like?"

"I'm going to be the guest singer at the Midnight Mass concert. My name will not be divulged. I will appear in costume and unmask myself after the last song. I plan on making Estelle proud. It won't give her back the years that she's lost or take all the pain away that she's suffered, but it will give her an enviable end to their alienation."

My cell phone interrupted our sharing. It was Father Paul, so I had to answer. It was ten thirty, which was late for a call, I thought. Something must be wrong.

"Hello, Father, is everything all right? Has something happened to Estelle?"

"Estelle wrote you another letter and was going to put it with the rest of the contents in the box. She called me in a panic when she saw that everything was gone."

"I have everything here with me. Oh, my, good God! What did you tell her?"

"I had to tell her the truth. I told her that I had given you the key a couple of months ago and that you had read everything and knew it all. I told her that we talked about everything, that we both cried and that you were okay. She asked me if that's what made you leave. She believes that you're not coming back. I went to the house immediately to reassure her that you had full intentions of returning, hopefully before Christmas. It took me a while to convince her, but when I left her, she seemed calmer. I will check on her tomorrow."

"It's too late for me to call her now, but I will make sure to call as soon as I get up tomorrow morning. Thank you for letting me know and for being there for us.

Father Paul, while I have you on the phone, I want to ask you a big favor. I want to be an invited mystery guest and give a Christmas concert during Midnight Mass. I would like you to start posting that there will be a special guest who will be singing. Give them any excuse for the changes to the program but don't reveal who is coming. Leave the rest to me. I will be in St Magloire by the 24th."

"That sounds wonderful! Yes. I will even start a rumor and drop a few names here and there to confuse everybody. This village needs a good stirring."

"Thanks again for calling, and I will be in touch with more details as I know them. Call me if you need me."

I called Estelle first thing in the morning. She sounded so small on the phone. I assured her that I would be home for Christmas. I then asked her if she would like to move in with me permanently. We had many years to cram into the time we had left. The strength in her voice came back as she said yes to my offer. I told her that we would talk it all out over a cup of tea and molasses cookies when I got back. The laughter in her voice was a gift to my heart. She said that she would have a double batch made for when I arrived. Estelle also told me that a special guest was going to sing at Midnight Mass and that she hoped that we could go together. I didn't commit. I said that we would have to see and that we would talk about it when I got home.

Patty agreed to help. We had less than two weeks left to charter a jet for the trip back to Quebec, pack, plan, and make sure we had a limo for a few days. I spoke to Father

Paul often to see if he had all his ducks in a row at his end and to tell him what I was doing at my end and what I would need for the concert. The acoustics were good in the church, but I wanted something spectacular! so that I would bring a professional-grade sound system along with my usual engineer. Though Billy was retired too, he was thrilled to give up his quiet Christmas alone and be a part of this event.

***

Everything was planned. We were all packed and ready to go. It was arranged that Patty and Billy would drive the limousine to the church from the airport and that they would stay at the rectory with Father Paul. That would intrigue the villagers. They would arrive two days before me to get everything set up and ready for the concert. My car was already at the airport. I had driven myself when I left for Nova Scotia. My flight landed in Levis at 11 am on the 24th. I got to my house at 12;30. Estelle was standing in the living room window when I pulled up to the driveway. The door swung open, and Estelle was in my arms, squeezing my neck like she would never let go. I held her tight myself. It was the warmest welcome I had ever received.

No sooner were we in the house; Estelle came out with a plate full of my favorite cookies and two large glasses of milk. She said that this was the way she had first served molasses cookies to me when I was two. It seemed fitting to have them this way again…with milk. I smiled at her and agreed with a mouth full of cookies.

After supper, I told Estelle I wanted to go say hello to Father Paul and bring him the gift I bought him. I knew that he liked the occasional cigar so I got him the best that I could find in Toronto. Patty opened the rectory door when I knocked. It was nice to see them all relaxed and comfortable with each other. I gave Father Paul his gift and in return, he passed out the cigars for our enjoyment. I stayed with them for an hour or so. I would be back at the church at ten thirty to set up and get dressed. Father Paul would find a reason for needing my presence at the rectory. We were all excited. This would be my best Christmas ever.

When I got back to the house, Estelle asked me if I would go to Midnight mass with her. I cheerfully agreed, knowing too well what was planned. The phone rang at quarter after nine. It was Father Paul asking if I would be so kind as to give him a hand. Sister Marie-Jacques was not well, and he didn't feel right leaving her alone during mass.

Estelle was disappointed that she had to attend the mass by herself. I told her that I would meet her there as soon as I could. She was okay with that. Estelle always sat near the back of the church. Just before the concert started, Patty went and got Estelle and brought her to the front pew to sit with her. There Patty put a lovely corsage on Estelle's blouse, telling her that it was from me. Estelle was dumbfounded, and the villagers had looks of puzzlement and some with disdain. Patty, on the other hand, had a smile from ear to ear.

The church was full to capacity with no standing room. The word of a star performance had reached the entire county and then some. The priest came out and welcomed everyone, and started the mass. After the first reading, which was of Jesus' birth in the manger, he then introduced the special guest.

"Ladies and gentlemen and precious little ones, it is my pleasure to introduce our guest with an angelic voice and generous heart, CiCi Pascale!"

I walked towards the altar, singing Ave Maria for my first song. I looked out at the crowd, who looked back at me in awe. I looked down at Estelle, and I could tell that tears were streaming down her face with a big smile on her lips. After my last song, I stood at the pulpit and addressed the crowd.

"I would like to thank you all for coming. It has been an honor to momentarily leave my retirement to perform this special concert for you. A concert special to me as well, which I would like to dedicate to Estelle Garand. For those of you who know of me, you also know that my identity has always been private and protected. A handful of people know who I am personally, mostly by necessity. It has been that way during my entire career. Tonight, however, I want to make a public reveal and remove my mask, which has sheltered and hidden me."

As I'm taking my mask off, I look towards Estelle, and I see that she is hardly breathing, and fear has replaced the smile on her face. I then continue to speak, which silences the murmuring of the crowd.

"I am Celine Thibault. I was born in St Magloire on February 4th, 1954. I am the daughter of Xavier Thibault and Estelle Garand. No explanation is needed or deserved. I am proud to be who I am. Estelle's daughter."

I looked at Father Paul, and I could see tears on his face as he smiled. I look at the congregation with a special leering glare towards Diane Menard as I walk down from the pulpit and over to Estelle. I offer her my hand and say loudly, "Come with me, Mother. Let's go home."

The hush in the church was deafening. The look on their faces was priceless. My head was held up and proud, and Estelle was a rag of tears holding onto my arm. As we were walking out arm in hand, a voice loudly called out Estelle's name. We both turned to see who it was. It was Claire, the nurse at the senior's home. With tears in her eyes, she simply said, "Estelle, I am so sorry."

Estelle nodded and looked at me, and we both looked at Claire and smiled, then turned and walked out of the church to our limousine, which was waiting to take us to the airport. Patty and Billy had gone to the home and packed Estelle's things, including my bassinet, and were waiting for us in the car out front. I looked at Estelle when I asked Patty to drive us to the house first. I wanted to get Mr. Pete. Then we drove to our awaiting chartered jet, which took us home to Nova Scotia.